The Ascenders
Return to Grace
Book 3
Monty Clayton Ritchings

Library and Archives Canada Cataloguing in Publication

Ritchings, Monty 1951 -

The Ascenders Return to Grace Book 3 ((paperback)

Monty C. Ritchings

ISBN: **978-0-9781891-6-7**

FAMOUS RELEVANT QUOTES

"If you want to fly, you have to give up what weighs you down."

Roy T. Bennett

"Change the way you look at things and the things you look at change."

Wayne Dyer

"Change is painful, but nothing is as painful as staying stuck somewhere you don't belong."

Mandy Hale

"Living your life based on your ancestral history is as valuable as getting stuck on a never ending merry-go-round."

Monty C. Ritchings

Chapter 1

"Everything looks so beautiful! The plants are so shiny, they are almost hard to look at."

"It is what happens when people care, my dear. Nature loves to give back like this. It is a natural connection."

Dawn and one of the other members were walking through the gardens, chatting. It was another wonderful day in Greenwood Commons.

"I guess we should find our way back. The meeting this morning is about our new children's program. This should be exciting, too."

"I would never have believed that life could be so good. If you had asked me a couple of years ago when everything was barren and all the people were so angry, I would have thought this was an impossible dream. We sure have to be thankful for those folks who got rid of all that bad energy. I wonder whatever happened to them."

"My feeling is that they are still around here somewhere, watching over us. Reverend Harry has sure developed an amazing relationship with them."

"And he grew so much, too. He is so much more now. It seems you just touch him now and whatever is bothering you disappears. Do you think this is what it was like when Master Jesus walked the earth?"

"I think so. It is so nice to be able to reach out to him, then watch the changes happen. Much of what we have been looking at during our walk today was his doing. We can often see him sitting on one of our park benches, looking like he is meditating. My suspicion is, he is chatting with the plant divas. Every time he does, whatever he is doing, the plants seem shinier, and they are so fragrant. Even plants I have never smelled before emit a beautiful perfume."

As they entered the cafeteria, all the residents were getting settled in. The meeting was about to start. A typical Saturday morning!

Since Greenwood Commons was a cohousing community, every resident was a board member.

Decisions were made by consensus, and not until it was attained. It was fortunate the game players had long been weeded out, so the meetings always flowed well. Each person attending wanted the best for everyone.

It was Dawn's turn to lead the meeting this day, since the focus was on the new children's gardening program.

"Good morning, my friends. It is my pleasure to lead this meeting this morning. We have some exciting new projects to begin now that spring is well underway.

Let's take a few moments to tune into the energies, so we all provide the best input into this session."

They had all done this process a hundred times, so it did not take long for the energies to rise to a suitable level. As they focused on their breaths, taking long slow breaths, moving their bellies to draw in the most air possible, they visualized gold energy emitting from their solar plexuses. The energy swirled through the room, joining the energies of all the others.

The combined energy spread its wings, reaching beyond the room, out into the gardens, throughout the town, the region, even reaching right out to the Cosmos.

Connecting with Source always felt so good!

As everyone returned, smiles that almost cracked the owner's face radiated throughout, shining so brightly, they made the sun jealous!

"The focus of today's meeting is about helping our children connect with the plant energies so they can learn to understand their relationship with nature itself.

My suggestion is that we build planter boxes in the patio area for raised box gardening. This will make it easy for the children to see how their gardens are growing rather than just letting them take part in looking after the bigger gardens."

One member jumped in right away, adding, "I knew this was your plan, so I took the liberty of ordering the materials from our board manufacturing plant. This way, we can get right to the work party this morning."

Another member added, "I have placed several wheel barrels of soil nearby. We should be able to have these boxes ready to plant this afternoon."

"Well, what are we sitting here for? Let's get to it. Meeting adjourned if all agree." Dawn was the first out the door.

Younger families comprised most of the people living in this community. Ever since the ordeal with the orb and all its offspring had been resolved, the birthrate had skyrocketed in this town.

Everyone had found peace here in this little town. The positive energy flowed everywhere. Reverend Harry still offered programs for personal evolution at the center. Teesha was still busy with all her yoga classes, too. It was easy to feel the love!

The town's economic health had soon been restored too when the Windsurfers arrived with their plans for the board plant. Who would have ever thought that a town could thrive on helping Mother Earth! Collecting and repurposing all the garbage plastic that was destined to be dumped into the waste stream (or trout streams) had saved the day.

Trucks arrived daily with loads of plastic. As quick as a wink, the liquefied plastic was mixed with sawdust or whatever other former waste was available. Then, the mixture like magic became building boards of any shape and size desired.

This day's lumber was created by laying many layers of strips of cardboard throughout the length of the mold. Adding the natural dye to the mixture made it almost impossible to tell these boards from the old ones made from cutting down and destroying trees. They would make great planter boxes!

The building party stood outside, assessing the location where the planters would live. Of course, there were plenty of yummy treats and drinks to fuel the workers.

Inclusion of the children was important to the adults, since this project was for them. Defining their jobs came first. There were ten large planter boxes and six small planters for smaller plants, like herbs. The parents let the children choose which they were moved to help with.

In a flash, there were many busy little beavers. Children could see what needed to be done. Soon, the parents found themselves in advisory roles as the children let their engineering skills come to life.

The younger children placed the bases where the planters would reside. Next, they helped put the side boards in place as the older children screwed and nailed each container together.

It only took a couple of hours for the project to be completed. All that needed to be done now was add the soil.

The children thought this would be a marvelous job for the parents since they felt they needed refreshments after such hard work! Like magic, watermelon smoothies were being swizzled down thirsty throats!

As the planting began, Dawn had the children stand around her. She explained the importance of creating the gardens.

"It is very important for us to know each of the plants. We need to know its name, why we are planting it, and who its friends are. Plants, like humans, need to share their lives with others who support them.

They also need to be placed where the environment is suitable for their ability to thrive.

In these smaller boxes, we are going to plant herbs. Do you know why we like to grow lots of different kinds of herbs? Anyone?"

Right away, the answers rang out. "Making supper yummy." "Making soaps." "Making the air smell nice." Everyone laughed and laughed. This was another good day.

"Now, when we plant, remember to give loving energy to the soil, to the plants and, to the environment surrounding. As we become one with the plants, they feel the love. This makes them want to grow nice and healthy. When they are ready, they will taste so much better than plants that are not treated as special.

Every day, we must come to visit them and share our energy by focusing on them. We must also energize the water before we bless them with it."

The children all stood in front of the planter they had helped construct. As they placed their hands over the containers, they projected gold energy to the soil and to the plants. They focused in their minds on how much they loved their friends in nature.

It was easy to see the plants respond to this loving attention. There will be some yummy veggies soon!!!

Chapter 2

"What are you doing, my dear?"

Suzie was standing looking into the fishpond. It was a cute little pond only about four feet round. She had a funny look on her face as her dad walked up to her.

"I am talking to the man." Suzie said, pointing at the pond.

"Really, there is a man in the pond, Suzie? What is he doing?" Dad was not sure what antics his daughter was up to this time. He knew she had quite an imagination and enjoyed making up stories, but he was aware enough that he did not want to make her stop telling her stories. Some of them were quite fanciful, but what child doesn't have imaginary friends or Unicorns at some point in their young lives?

"He is real, daddy. He was talking to me. Honest. He told me to tell you that everyone needed to be careful. Situations are developing that might cause us problems if we do not pay heed. What does heed mean, daddy?"

At that, daddy stepped forward and looked into the pool. All he saw were a few kois kibbitzing about in the water. Regardless, what his daughter stated demanded attention. That was not the kind of information that a five-year-old comes up with.

"Have you spoken with him before, Suzie?

"Uh-huh."

"How many times have you spoken with him? Does he always say the same thing to you?"

"Every time I come to the pool; he is here. He says the same words every time. That is why I know what to say to you. I am not afraid of him. I just like looking at him."

"Well, you keep talking with him and I will see if I can find out what he is warning us about."

With that, dad and daughter turned and walked together into the main building of Greenwood Commons. Daughter headed off to find friends, while dad went in search of some other grownups. This man in the pool seemed to be far more than his daughter's fertile imagination.

Bumping into Dawn, he smiled at her, saying. "My daughter has just had a really weird experience. I need to find someone to talk with to see if we can figure out what is going on."

After he had told her the story, Dawn suggested he go see Rose at the community center in town.

Rose was sitting in the cafeteria with a group of people when Dave walked in. As soon as he spied Rose, he walked right over to her table.

Sensing the urgency, Rose removed herself from the group by standing up.

"Sorry to intrude, Rose, but I need to talk with you about something that is going on. I spoke with Dawn. She suggested you were the one to see if you could make some sense of this."

Rose guided Dave over to another table. Sitting down, she patted the seat of the chair beside her, saying, "Tell me."

She gave him her full attention as he told the story. "I know my daughter has a healthy imagination, but she told me she has spoken to a man in the koi pool several times over the past few days. He says the same thing every time.

"Thank you Dave. I will see what I can find out. This does sound mysterious. I am glad you took the time to fill me in. I will let you know what I find out."

With that, Dave got up and left. Rose sat and focused for a few moments, trying to connect with the story. As she contemplated, she moved into Rachel mode searching for an answer... and there it was!

As Dave wheeled into the parking lot of the cohousing site, he noticed several people sitting on the grass. They were meditating, or so he thought.

As he pulled up, they stood up and ran over in front of his car. He slammed on his brakes, narrowly missing hitting them.

These were people he had never met before, which was odd because he thought he knew everyone for miles. One of these people walked up to his window. She looked very angry.

"We are here to tell you people to get off our land. This land has been our traditional land for thousands of years. You are trespassing, now get off."

Dave tried to say something back to the woman, but she just turned with the others and returned to sitting on the grass.

Very shaken, Dave continued to his parking spot, then ran into the main building. He did not have to look far for someone to talk with, as there was already a meeting happening.

"I take it you just got accosted too, hey Dave?" said one lady sitting at the table.

"Yah, what the heck is this all about? This sounds serious. We have all worked so hard to build a wonderful home here for our families and friends. Now they are telling us to get off their lands. Who are these people?"

"We don't know, but Rose is on her way over to help. She has some news for us that may help."

A few minutes later, Rose appeared at the door. She looked very concerned.

"I guess your daughter's man in the pool was right. We do need to take heed. I did some checking as soon as you left. It seems the government is promoting the aboriginal people to reclaim their lands, so they have posted people in front of any large buildings and residential projects. Their goal is to intimidate anyone they can.

They have the courts on their side, so these people are pushing hard to take what they can. This only happened a few days ago, but there are already several cases fighting the order in front of the Supreme Court."

"I am not one to fight with people. I feel we should all strive to get along and share, but I will not stand by and have my home taken away from me. Where were these people before we started to build? Why didn't the city government that gave us this property know this land belonged to these people, as they claim?" Dave asked.

Another member spoke. "I agree with you, Dave. We have been sitting here asking these questions ourselves. We will be making a visit to city hall tomorrow to see what we can find out... and, more importantly, what we can do about this."

The following morning, a contingency from Greenwood Commons was sitting in front of the mayor's desk. He was aware of the situation but had not taken it seriously, as he thought they would quash it in court before the news got out to the street.

With everyone present, he picked up the phone, contacting his local government representative. The answering machine was all he got.

"I will continue trying to get some answers. Maybe you folks should reach out wherever you can as well and try to find out anything. All I know is they incorporated this city on the land it holds today over two hundred years ago. No one has ever made such a preposterous claim before. There just is not a precedent."

The next stop was at the community center. Rose, Harry, and Teesha were in the conference room. As the six arrived, they were invited to join in their session.

Rose suggested that Rachel would like to weigh in on this situation, so they all went quiet, focusing on their breath.

Soon after, Rachel appeared. Although she smiled with love at each of her friends, she had a very serious demeanor.

"Our friend in the pool was very serious. Trouble is here. However, when there is trouble, there is also the opportunity for growth and healing.

The government people are up to their tricks again. They have spent all the money they can get their hands on. In order to forestall bankruptcy, they have opted to create this disturbance. Their plan is to let the aboriginal people take the fall for their dishonesty.

These people have been riled up for a fight, and the government people are capitalizing on it. The timing was right and now they are not going to back down.

Our job is to settle them down on the mundane level for the interim while we intervene on the spiritual level. There will be some major changes occur, but stay put and do not let them intimidate you. We need peaceful and open dialogue."

Once Rachel had returned to her home in the spheres, Rose reconvened the meeting.

"I think we should be nice to these people sitting in front of our homes, but, at the same time, we should not give an inch. I have some lawn chairs they can sit on and maybe we can rustle up a table for them as well. They might as well make themselves comfortable during their long stay. It might be awhile."

Everyone agreed with Dawn's suggestions right away. This would at least give them some time to figure out a plan. Once the discussion closed, the people from the cohousing community returned home.

Harry spoke right away. "We need intervention from a higher source. I am sensing a tremendous opportunity for healing for everyone. Any suggestions?"

"Good morning everyone!" Goose said.

"I don't know how many times you have scared me with your entrances, Goose, but it is a relief to see you and the Windsurfers here this morning," Harry said.

"Well, you asked for suggestions, so we took that as our cue to join you. This situation sounds just like the kind of job that is right up our alley."

Chapter 3

The Windsurfers stood in front of the pond. Beside them was Suzie and her dad. They all stared into the pool, hoping the man would reappear. A couple of raging koi flopped about in a very ordinary-looking fish bowl was all they saw.

"Are you thinking what I am thinking, Goose?" asked Condor.

"Yep. Time for a swim."

Preparing to dive into the pool, Suzie announced she was going too, and at that she dove headfirst into the water ahead of the others. Her dad stood there in shock as his little girl disappeared into the depths of what used to be a three foot deep pool of water.

"No time to waste now. Let's catch up with her," said Raven as he followed Suzie into the water.

Dave stood, still in shock, as the rest of the group dove deep into the water. It did not even enter his mind to question how eight grown people and his daughter could dive into a four foot wide, three foot deep pool of water and just disappear.

The pool looked as serene as ever as Dave continued standing there in shock.

The water was not cold. They swam and swam, searching for the bottom. In their minds, each of the Windsurfers hoped Suzie could hold her breath long enough to get to wherever they were headed. They did not have a problem, since they could breathe underwater easily, just by believing they were fish.

Suzie was just far enough ahead that they could see her, but they did not try to catch up. She seemed to know where she was heading, so they let her lead.

It seemed to take forever. They swam and swam with what seemed no end in sight. They had traveled down what seemed like forever, but now were swimming across in what appeared to be a large cave. There was enough room for them to swim on, but that was all they did. Just swim. They had all now concluded that Suzie was no ordinary Homo Sapien.

It was a full two hours before Suzie reached dry land. It was a craggy beach with little place for one to pull themselves ashore. Being a tiny little sprite, she waited in the water for the others to catch up.

As heads popped out of the water, they all stared at their new situation.

Suzie moved close to the shore. Goose could see that she would have trouble pulling herself up onto the beach, so he moved behind her and lifted her up far enough so she could grasp a large rock and pull herself onto the beach. The others followed suit, soon creating what in another world would appear to be a bunch of logs cast ashore by the high tide.

They lay there for a long time, saying nothing. Laying there, just letting themselves recuperate from the long swim was all they wanted.

If that was not a world record for the longest underwater swim without breathing apparatus, then the records people were allowing fish into the competition!

They were all sitting up on the beach now. It was time to make a plan, if that was possible. As they sat looking at the scenery, they pondered to themselves, how could they make a plan if no one had any idea where they were, who they wanted to meet or...?

Suzie looked at the others. "My dad would tell me I could not come with you if I asked him, so I jumped in and saved him the bother. No matter what, I knew I needed to be part of this. I need to meet the man who was talking to me."

"How did you know we would follow you?" asked Raven. "People don't just jump into pools to do deep diving every day."

"I could read your energy. You all looked like fish standing there, so I knew you were joining me. I also knew you were supposed to help me figure out what was going on."

"You are pretty smart for a little girl. Do you have anything else you would like to share with us?" asked Goose.

"I enjoy being a little girl, so for now I will stay in this form. I think it will be helpful in our near future. You will come to know more later. For now, let's figure out why we are here."

With that, each of the nine members of this entourage stood up and shook themselves off, so they did not look like they had been swimming in their clothes for hours, and set off... to somewhere.

They had walked for several hours, stopping to have picnics along the way. Goose just did not like going hungry, and, with the obvious lack of catering trucks in the area, he waved his hands before himself, conjuring up some yummy treats and drinks for himself and his friends to enjoy along the way. The others could have created their own treats, but Goose enjoyed it so much, they let him provide... and that he did. What is it about mini-donuts?

The walk was not difficult, as the terrain was quite flat. Although they found themselves deep in a heavily wooded forest, they found a path. They followed along, trusting it was where they needed to be. As they walked, they kept calm and connected to Source, enjoying their afternoon stroll as they shared some trail songs!

They walked for more than a day before anything interesting appeared before them. Even the wild animals stayed in hiding. They were all alone (well, except for the trees waving at them!)

A bit of a climb brought them to an area that manifested into a most spectacular view. It was a lovely valley large enough that it would take a day to walk across it. Something caught their eye though. Something more than the gentle beauty of an undisturbed land.

It was smoke! Then they realized it was several pillars of smoke plumed up into the air. There was a village in the valley. They had reached a settlement! But who lived there? And where were they? (Another question they might also have asked was: When were they?)

"Let's stop and meditate for a few minutes, so when we join these people with our energies, they are as high as possible. We want to project as positive an energy field as possible. And maybe we should have a little nourishment as well," Goose said, as he sat down on a little knoll.

A few minutes later, Papi said, "I think I should get into butterfly and go do some reconnaissance. That way, we will know what to expect."

"Maybe you could just say hi to me!" a voice said from behind a rock. It shocked them as a young woman walked into their view. They had not even sensed her presence.

"I am Portu, the gatekeeper for our tribe. I have been watching you as you walked along our trail. What are mini-donuts?"

Everyone laughed as Portu came to sit on a rock with them. Goose, of course, conjured up some mini-donuts for everyone to share. Portu smiled as she took another coconut one.

"Mmmm. These are good. May I have the recipe she said?" She laughed as she conjured up her own version of mini-donuts.

"Anyway, what brings you folks here? We do not get very many visitors."

Suzie told her the story of the man in the pool and how they had dove into the pool, swimming down deep into the water for hours in search of him.

"I am not sure who he might be, but I am sure he will show up when the time is right. Come to our village. You can stay with us while you figure out why you are here."

It took about another hour to walk to the village. The scenery was breathtaking. The trees glistened in the sunlight. Beneath the trees were all kinds of berries. Salmonberries, blackberries, huckleberries and even some none of them knew. They all hung deliciously tempting.

Amazing how even the wild animals now came to say hi to the new humans. Rabbits scurried alongside the trail while coyotes lazed in grassy patches uninterested in their mobile meals scurrying by. Have you ever seen a coyote smile? It was a joyful time!

The village was quite large. There were about twenty structures made from wood and sod. They looked very comfortable.

"This is our summer home. In the winter we return to the big water where it is warmer and there are plenty of fish to sustain us. You arrived almost at the same time as we did," Portu said.

Portu ushered her new friends into the center of the village as people rushed over to see the new comers. Everyone smiled. They felt so welcome.

Once the pleasantries were over, they led the Windsurfers to a building. Portu told them they could make themselves at home and rest.

It was pleasant inside. There was an enormous pile of comfy looking pelts in the corner, so they each grabbed a few and flopped onto the floor. They arranged themselves so they could face each other. No one wanted to rest, but they sure wanted to have a private chat.

"So where are we? Anybody got an idea?" asked Raven.

"I think the better question is when are we?" answered Condor. "Have you noticed there are no modern tools? They make everything they use from stone. It feels like we have stepped back in time a little."

"If that is true, then they will not know when, now is. After all, time is relative. How do you think we can figure it out? pondered Suzie.

They all looked at her, shocked. Who would think a five-year-old girl could even think up such a concept?

"Just saying. Maybe we need to ask a higher source," Suzie added.

In an instant, guess who appeared? Rachel, of course.

"I Ii Suzic! It is nice to see you again." Rachel spoke to Suzie like they were old friends. The smirk on her face betrayed her, though, but did not answer the question about Suzie's real identity.

The issue at home is that the government appears to be using the aboriginal people as pawns to stir up trouble. They are using them to hide the fact that they have squandered all the country's money. Our mission is to heal the hearts and minds of these people so they cannot be used as pawns in the future. We will deal with the government people later.

Suzie has led you to a time before these people even existed here. Portu and her community are the earliest form of humans found in this region. They precede the aboriginals.

Your mission is to understand their society. Later, when you move forward in time, you will encounter these aboriginal people and help them deal with the foreigners when they arrive.

After all, an ounce of prevention, in this case, is worth a ton of mending.

Chapter 4

L ife in Portu's community was quite serene. Everyone knew their job and fulfilled it to the best of their skills. The men hunted while the women collected berries and other wild plants as they looked after their children.

The nine visitors blended into their new community. They never even questioned why all the Windsurfers could speak their language. It just seemed so natural speaking to them. It was almost like they were cousins from the other side of the mountain.

"Have you noticed how they all go to their houses around the same time every day?" Goose asked as they were all laying on their beds one day.

"Yes. I also noticed they always say a prayer when they head off to hunt or pick berries. They seem to appreciate every bit of the bounty they have received. I think it would be special to meet with them so we can learn about them and their traditions. Let's see if we can set that up," said Condor.

"I wonder how they would feel if Papi and I let out our inner aspects. I really want to go for a fly! How about you Papi?" asked Hummingbird.

Papi laughed as she admitted she had already gone on a few secret flights. "I followed the men hunting one day. Curiosity got the best of me!. Even though they were killing my friends, they did it with such respect. The animal they caught willing died for them, so I did not feel sad."

As they prepared the meat to bring it home, they did prayers and washed the area with special smoke. I think they were sending the soul of the animal on its way to the light.

They brought home every piece of the animal to use except for a small amount of meat, which they left on the spot. I stayed after they left to see what would happen with this meat.

Soon after they left, a group of coyotes sauntered up to the meat. They hunched down on the ground with their forepaws stretched out toward the meat. They looked at their prize but stayed in this position for several minutes. A sound came from one of the older coyotes. Then they all stood, and in silence, ate their meal. No wonder the coyote had no interest in the rabbits on the trail!

"Even the animals are in sync with the Cosmic here. If these people at home are their descendants, what could have happened?" asked Raven.

A few days later, Portu told them there would be a festival that night. The elders invited them to join in. They gave each member of the Windsurfers (including Suzie) clothing similar to the members of Portu's community.

At the fire that night, the elder initiated each of them into the community .

"You are now members of our family. Even though the wind will take you elsewhere, just as it brought you to us, we consider you kindred spirits. May the light always shine for you on your journey. You are welcome to be with us for as long as you choose.

We knew you were kindred spirits because you could see our smoke on the day you arrived. If you were not akin to us, you would not have seen the smoke, as it is only visible to people who can vibrate at our frequency. Thank you for joining us."

Once the ceremony was over, everyone gathered near the fire. The elders of the community sat with the Wind Surfers to tell them stories of their ancients.

"We ascended here from a planet that had run its course. It could no longer nourish our bodies. Spirit planted our seeds on this planet for us to thrive. Our only job was to share love with the resources of this planet. We have learned to be grateful.

We have decided to adopt all nine of you because we know you also know the power of grace. We have also seen that you are here to help remove a great blight from the future of mankind on this planet.

Our sages have told us that, at some point in the future, humans will be given the opportunity to step away from the cradle of the Cosmic to establish a higher level of consciousness. They say there will be lessons.

Chapter 5

And time did pass by. The Wind Surfers lived with their new family for many years, learning and embracing the truths of life beyond ego.

One day, as the men returned from hunting, some visitors greeted them. The new generation of humans had arrived. They wore beautiful clothing made from the skins of animals they had consumed along the way. Their outfits were much more adorned than Portu's people wore. The decorations told stories about their journey.

"Welcome, my friends. Come into our village and make yourself at home. Rest from your long journey." Portu beckoned the visitors to sit by the main fire.

"We have been expecting you, so we have constructed new buildings for you to live in. Please make use of them as you wish."

The visitors struggled with the language Portu spoke, but understood her gestures. They felt awkward and unsure as they moved toward the buildings.

The Wind Surfers came to the rescue as they understood the situation. They joined the new people at the fire, spreading themselves around between them. When they spoke to them in their own language, rather than smiling, the visitors became even more uncomfortable.

As each member tried to build a conversation, they realized it was futile. These people were not of the same ilk as their hosts. Now they needed to investigate what these people had on their minds.

The energy at the fire became quite low as no one spoke. They just sat staring at the fire. After a while, the guests rose, bowed to their hosts, and went to their assigned houses.

Looking at the Elder, who had a questioning look on his face, Goose said to Condor, "We had better find out what these folks are up to before there are any problems."

Condor then said, "Let's get invisible and slip into their house. I know it isn't polite to eavesdrop, but I agree. We need a heads up. Let's talk with the elder and let him know."

A while later, Condor and Goose sat by the fire with the Elder.

"It seems that they do not know how to accept the hospitality you have provided. They feel you are going to expect something from them they may not be willing to give. One fellow said he was worried you would want to learn how they hunt so well.

It seems they may not stay for long as the pressure they feel from their fears will drive them onward."

"Just as my guidance suggested. These people may be evolved enough to see our smoke, but they still live their lives based on fear. I will seek guidance from Spirit." The elder rose at that moment, concluding the conversation.

Several uncomfortable days later, the visitors announced they were continuing their journey in search of a new home. At that, they turned away from their hosts, picked up their belongings and were gone, with not even a word of thanks.

As they walked away, the elder made signs of forgiveness to them, then offered them peace and prosperity. The offering went unnoticed.

"Sounds like we had better keep an eye on these folks. I would have thought they would have appreciated the grace bestowed upon them," Papi said as she prepared herself for a little espionage.

"I am coming too," said Songbird. "It's been a long time since I had some fun. Are you coming, Hummingbird?"

And with that, the three of them become their alter egos and were off. Songbird and Hummingbird were so excited about going on this mission, everyone else could see them flipping over and over in the air and doing deep dives. Everyone laughed.

It was a good thing the three were now very comfortable holding themselves in their animal form. They watched the visitors trudge along for three days before the newcomers announced they had found a suitable home.

The elder sat with Goose, Condor and Raven at the campfire.

He said, "They have forgotten themselves. With the generations of walking from their homeland, they have been so focused on surviving they have forgotten themselves."

"What can we do to help them?" asked Condor.

"Let's wait for Papi and her friends to get back so we know where they are, then we can make a plan. In the meantime, I am going to go meditate and see what comes to me."

Condor was sitting alone at the fire meditating as the trio popped in. He looked at Papi, as he settled his heart back down, and said, "It does not matter that we can all pop in and out as we please. It still scares the heck out of me when someone pops in unexpectedly."

He laughed and gave Papi as big a hug as one can give a person who you can almost carry in your pocket. Then he mussed up Songbird's and then Hummingbird's hair.

"What did you learn?" asked Condor. "Wait just a minute, I will go get the others, so you don't have to repeat yourself."

A few minutes later, everyone gathered at the fire. Papi started in.

"They have found a place to settle that is about three days' walk from here. It is a pleasant valley with a huge stream, so it should be a good place for them. We stayed long enough to listen as they spoke about their plans. It seems that some will make this a permanent camp while others will rest and carry on. They did not say where these others will go. It almost seems like they feel homeless and unable to settle."

The elder then said, "I know the place where they are. We have used it for a hunting camp before. They will like it there. I received a message while I was meditating. I was told to keep our energy up for now so they cannot find their way back here. If they come by here, they will not see us, as the frequency will be too high. I have already adjusted it.

There will be lessons soon that will provide these people the opportunity to choose to know themselves again. If they choose to work through the lessons, they will see us again as their energy rises. However, if they choose to stay in their current condition, they will find their lives very challenging. We can only wait and see."

It did not take long for them to find out the choice these people had made. Portu's community continued with their daily lives. One day, they observed people watching them, or more correctly, searching for where they thought they might be. Since they could not see them, it was apparent they had chosen the lower choice.

"We need to find these people," the man said to his followers. "We need their food and tools so we can survive. They have to be here somewhere."

It was quite challenging for the Wind Surfers to keep from laughing as these people walked right through the camp without being able to see it. It was easy to see on their face they had memorized the trail they had traveled but they could not find the camp.

After a moment, they continued on with confused looks on their faces. Later that day, they walked right through again as they made their way back.

"We would have helped them out by sharing our food and tools with them had they asked," said Portu. "We have all we need and more. The Universe has provided us well.

Now they will need to work things out for themselves so they can learn from their choices. If they only understood, the longer they focus on the lower energy of stealing from us, the more struggle they will endure. However, we have been instructed to leave them to their lessons."

The Wind Surfers offered to check in on them regularly. They hoped the people would realize their lower thinking was holding them back, but it seemed every time one of them listened in, it was the same old story.

Suzie suggested they provide them with some inner guidance. "If we were to plant some good thoughts in their heads, maybe they would shift their thinking."

"Can you do that, Suzie?" asked Goose with an inquiring eye. He was getting an idea who Suzie really was.

"We just need to cause a distraction, then I can connect with that person's mind. Let's try it with their leader. After all, he is the most influential. If we can sway him, then we have a chance of getting them all on board."

Papi flipped into her butterfly and headed to the camp. She knew who she was looking for. Since this was important, she only took a couple of seconds to reach him.

Arriving there, she saw him right away. She flitted over to him as if she was looking for a flower to light on and plopped herself down on his arm. It did the trick. However, he knocked Papi right off his arm, yelling obscenities as if a bear had licked him.

Papi had braced for the knock, so she didn't get hurt, but she got herself back to the other camp fast.

Suzie had success! She had connected with the man. Pouring words of comfort first to him, then suggesting they meditate and pray to find a solution to their problem, she held his mind for about five minutes. When she let go, she accidentally said out loud, "Where have I felt that energy before?"

Realizing her faux pas, she looked at the others to find if they had heard her. They had. They were all smiling like Cheshire cats. One might say the cat (Cheshire or not) was out of the bag!

"Hi Guys!" she said as she transformed into Merle. "I always wanted to be a little girl, so when Dave and his wife became pregnant, I grabbed at the chance. It is so fun! I am not done yet." At that, Merle returned to be Suzie.

Everyone stood staring at her with a loving but incredulous look. Suzie just smiled and went off to play with the other little girls.

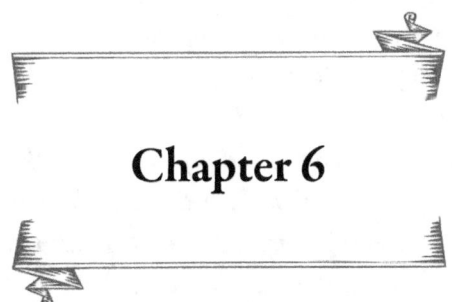

Chapter 6

Suzie's attempt at connecting with the leader had worked... sort of. The leader realized things were not right with his people. He decided to go have some quiet time, hoping he could come up with a workable solution.

The people were finding food, but it was not easy. This territory they were now living in provided different plant life than they had known previously. This was a problem because vegetation was a big part of their diet. The animals were the same, so they could provide enough meat for each member to survive. However, an excessive diet of dense protein was not their usual fare. The members were all suffering from constipation. Being they were grumpy anyway, since they had forgotten who they were inside themselves, they had become quite intolerable to each other.

The leader meditated and prayed, asking for help for his people. This was challenging to do. Trying to focus on connecting with the Universe when the body is yelling about its own concerns!

However, in time, he succeeded.

As he meditated, a brilliant light glowed in his mind. It soon spoke to him.

"I am Rachel. I serve the Universal God that created this earth and all that exists. I invite you to join me in this moment of knowing yourself through the eyes of God."

The leader smiled in recognition. He had never conferred with Rachel before. Deep inside, he felt a distant memory of her energy, likely from a previous lifetime.

"Your people have been traveling for so long, they have forgotten themselves and their connection with Source. The condition they have projected in their bodies is not from having too much dense protein. The ego causes this condition as it holds control of their lives. They have become stuffed up because they are too self-contained.

In order to fix this situation on the mental side, it is essential that you teach your members to reconnect. Once this happens, life will flow again.

Those who follow your leadership, if you choose to follow my advice, will find a happy home here on this land and will develop a strong bond with Portu's family. Those who choose not to take this advice would be best to continue journeying on. I hope that a good long walk will settle their body issues satisfactorily."

At that, Rachel smiled and disappeared, leaving the leader to continue in his meditation.

Rachel was right. He had been feeling the calling in his body for quite some time. He was now prepared to help his people reconnect.

Later in the day, he called all the people to the main fire. It was time to let each of them decide.

"I have meditated on our current problem and have received an answer. I will put this offer forward for each of you to choose for yourself what your future will look like.

The reason, I am told, for our current condition of constipation is because of our long outstanding choice to not connect with Source. We have disconnected with our own true heritage. In order to correct the situation, we should return to our ancient practice of connecting with Source regularly. Through this connection, it will guide us to fulfill our lives.

This is your choice. Those of you who choose to comply with these suggestions may stay and live here in this valley. Those who are not feeling the pull to comply, you are free to continue your journey. I am told the walk will do you well.

Although this is not a frivolous decision or one to make light of, you must make it right now. Those of you who wish to continue your journey must leave now."

At that point, the leader rose and retreated to his tent. The members sat and stared at each other. Before long, several members rose. Returning to their camp, they packed their minimal possessions and turned away from the main camp.

It was quiet in camp that night. Over half of the members had packed and left. The rest felt an odd quiet, like a new life was beginning. It was odd, but it was rejuvenating.

The leader led the members in a meditation. As they settled in, a bright light shone forth in their minds. They felt an excitement, a connection they had long forgotten.

A beautiful woman stood before them. Her long blond hair blowing in the breeze, adorned in a beautiful lavender gown. At once, they remembered.

"I am Rachel. I serve the Universal God that created this earth and all that exists. I invite you to join me in this moment of knowing yourself through the eyes of God."

The leader smiled again. He knew he had made the right choice.

"It gives me great pleasure to come to you at this time. Now is the time for you to remember the love you once shared with yourselves, the land and the Universe.

By making the choice to stay, you will share in the abundance created by making this decision.

In order to assist you in settling into your new home, I have invited my friend to help you relearn the plants of this region."

With that, she turned. A man stepped forward, dressed in the same beautiful garments they had worn during their travel. The beads and other adornments showed he was a powerful warrior.

"This is my friend, Klum. He will help you come to know this land. He will also teach you how to give thanks and respect to the land and the abundance it provides."

From that day forward, there was only joy in this new group that had found their way home. The meditation performed each night reconnected them with the true spirit of their people.

Klum enjoyed returning to human form so the people could embrace his knowledge as they wandered throughout the local region. It felt so good to him to feel his feet solid on the earth once again.

"Now that you have allowed yourself to let go of the stuffiness of your old life, you will still need to purge your body of unnecessary contaminants. Take a deep breath. Do you smell the fragrance of the Cascara tree?

If you do, let it lead you to itself. It wants to help you feel your best. When you find the tree, place your hand on it and wait for me."

Within minutes, everyone had their hand placed on a tree.

"Smell the bark. Is this the smell you could smell before? If it is, place both your hands on the bark. Think of the tree, sending it love and thanks for a few minutes. Now take your knife, placing it across the bark. Dig the blade in with a gentle motion, then push up. This will release a piece of the bark for you.

Once done, place your hand on the wound and see it healed."

They all smiled and yelled in delight when they removed their hands from the tree. It was like they had never touched it, and yet, they had a sizable piece of the bark in their hands.

On their return to the camp, Klum instructed them to fill a pot with water and bring it to a boil on the fire. At that point, they all placed their piece of bark in the water.

After steeping it for a while, they all drank a cup of the tea.

Faces smiled the next day. It had lifted a weight from their life.

"There are so many plants in the forest that have been created to help you keep yourself in perfect health. Listen to the quiet voice inside you when you walk. Look at the plants by stopping and focusing on each plant. Let it tell you its story. In time, you will have an entire store to enjoy."

Portu and her family came by often. They could all see each other again. Soon they were all like cousins, sharing their lives and their secrets to abundance. They learned to hunt while giving respect to the animals and to Mother Nature. The Universe provided them well.

Chapter 7

"What are we going to do about these people loitering around the end of our driveway?" asked a member of Greenwood Commons.

This question was on the minds of every person in the community. Tensions were growing as both sides resisted giving in to the other.

A meeting was called, and of course, everyone attended (because that is the way of life in Cohousing!). A functional plan needed to be put in place. There had to be a win-win for everyone.

Being that this was a sensitive situation, Reverend Harry and Rose joined in the meeting. This was a good idea because they had the answer. Most of the members had attended various courses at the center and embraced the philosophy that Harry espoused. However, few of them had evolved far enough to understand the value of working with Universal energy. Today, they would learn a valuable lesson.

It was Rose who led the conversation. "So we can create a win-win situation, we need to make the energy on both sides positive. We also need to make the folks on both sides of the problem feel they have been valued.

The real perpetrator of this situation is the government. They are depending on the others to feel they have been deprived of something to rile them up. If we can help them see the falsity of their position, maybe they will calm down.

We need to reset the energy before we can approach them so we can understand this situation. We need to draw them into our energy, so they become part of our community. To facilitate this, we need to make them feel wanted and comfortable out in the front driveway by bringing them chairs, tables, food, etc. given in kindness and love.

As we do this, we also need to do an energy exercise, bringing them into our energy fold. It is a simple exercise but very effective if everyone here is on board to take part. Everyone in favor?"

Raising their hands, every person agreed. Some were not sure what they were going to do, but they did not want to be the wrench that jammed the gears.

Rose smiled and looked at Harry as she invited him to present the visualization.

"Everyone sit in a comfortable position in your chair and focus on your breath with your eyes closed. Focus on your breath until you feel relaxed.

The next step is to feel your own energy field. Expand your energy and visualize it becoming stronger with each breath. Do this for a couple of minutes.

Now, see your energy expand into the room and integrate with the energies of all the others in the room. Follow your breath and keep visualizing the energy merging into one.

Now, see this combined energy rise beyond the roof of this building. See it spread to form an energy dome that covers all the property in Greenwood Commons from the road to the back of the property and to both sides. Make sure you include the area where the others are to be found.

Let the energy increase. Fill it with all the Universal love you can imagine. Hold the energy for as long as you can. Let the dome become a permanent fixture over our home, filling all with love.

Once you have completed the visualization, relax and enjoy the quiet for a few moments. When you are ready, open your eyes."

Once they had finished the meeting, everyone moved on to whatever they needed to do. Some went back to their homes, while some went for walks. They all stayed away from the front gate for a while just to let the effects of the visualization settle in.

As good visualizations always do, the effect was immediate and impactful. As people walked outside, they saw the people at the gate facing into the property. (Most of the time, they sat on the ground facing the road, scowling.) They were smiling. In fact, a couple of them were doing some kind of dance, like they were celebrating.

Dave was the first one to venture forth to interact with them. He was prepared. With him, he carried a large basket of food and drinks he planned to give to them.

As he walked to the end of the driveway, they all moved toward him, smiling and holding their hands out in welcome. He smiled as he approached, holding out the basket.

"I have brought you a picnic. It is a gift from everyone here. We want you to be comfortable. Soon, others will bring out comfy chairs and tables for you to enjoy."

As other tenants arrived right behind Dave, the people on the street offered them a seat so they could join them. Soon, it was a picnic to remember. Every person in Greenwood Commons was now present. More food arrived. Too bad the Wind Surfers were off on their mission.

Or were they?

Never to miss an opportunity to play, the Wind Surfers could feel the party coming together, so they projected home... and the party began... and as usual, never stopped for days!

Chapter 8

Much time had passed since their arrival. Many of the newcomers had married into Portu's family. They were now one big happy group, having accepted their new life based in Universal love.

It was an auspicious time for all. The people, the trees, the land, the animals, and the plants glistened as love abounded. Life was good!

Those who had walked away so long ago had survived as well. Their lives were not as glorious as those in Portu's village. If the truth be told, their lives were quite difficult.

Hunger was not something they had ever known before. It was an unfamiliar and unpleasant experience; one they would rather not have had to endure. Winter was coming in a few months. They did not know winter, so they did not know how to prepare. Hunger was to become a regular visitor.

Having arrived at Portu's village in the spring, they thought they had found the greatest place on earth. Hunting was plentiful. Soon saskatoon berries dangled on bushes in the forest, making them salivate as they waited for them to ripen. They hoped that meant blackberries were coming soon too. The clincher was that clean water was abundant. What more could one want?

But they had chosen to leave.

After leaving Portu's village, they traveled for many months before they found somewhere suitable to settle. They had traveled inland, far from the sea. This made the climate more challenging, as the ocean breezes did not smile on them. The summers were hot; the winters were cold... and long.

Their traditional style of their new homes was fine for spring and summer, but coming into late fall; they experienced something unfamiliar... cold.

It was fortunate they were familiar with fire, so they thought that building bigger fires would keep them warm, then they built fires inside their homes. This worked for a while until the snow got too deep. They could not find enough firewood to keep the fires burning.

As the snow fell deeper and deeper, the animals disappeared as well. Life was very dismal. Some of the older and less healthy members passed on from the cold and starvation. Those who survived became very bitter. How could life be so cruel?

Time was not their friend, nor was the weather. As they lay starving in their beds, they heard a noise outside. They could not move.

It sounded like others!

They knew of no others except Portu and her family. But their camp was far away from here, and they did not know where they had settled.

It must be someone else, they concluded.

It did not take long to find out. A strange person was standing in their doorway. This person stared at them for a moment, taking in the view. He then turned and walked away. They stayed on their beds, unable to move.

Outside, the newcomers gathered to discuss their findings. It seemed like an eternity to the people in the homes.

The newcomers prepared soup for them from packs they carried with them. They nursed the people for days until they were well enough to return to a somewhat normal version of life.

The newcomers tried to speak to these people, but they spoke in an unfamiliar language. However, they soon understood when the newcomers lined all of them up and forced them to travel with them.

Their new home was no more.

Hoping the newcomers would help them learn how to survive in this climate, they dreamed of beginning a new, good life with plenty of food, so they would have the strength to hunt and fish. This was not their lot.

Traveling for many days, the strangers forced them to walk in the deep, cold snow. They shivered as they trudged ahead with not enough clothing, and only minimal food. The only thoughts on their mind were questions about their future. Where were they going? What was going to happen to them?

After many days of struggling, before them, they saw a village ahead as they traveled down a steep slope into a plush valley. This must be their destination, they hoped. It was.

Their captors sat them down on the snowy ground. They left a few people to keep guard over them. The leaders continued into the town. They returned a while later, with others.

As they arrived, the group began having a heated discussion. It was obvious they were the center of the discussion. If only they could understand!

Soon, the leaders of the two groups disappeared back into the village. When they returned, their captors were smiling.

The people remained seated as their captors turned and walked away. What were all those furs they carried on their backs? They would never know.

The villagers, under orders of their leader, pulled the captives to their feet, forcing them to continue the walk into town. On arrival, they were all thrust into an old wood shed that looked like it could fall down any time. Once inside, the door slammed behind them and locked.

No one returned to see them for hours. They were hungry, and they were cold. They did not understand what was happening.

These new people kept them in the shed for many weeks, feeding them and keeping them somewhat comfortable. No one stayed with them or tried to tell them anything. They could not understand what was going on or what was going to happen to them. Although they now felt better, having eaten sufficient food, blankets and, a good fire for warming up, the tension of not knowing what lay in their future worried them.

One day, long after time had left them behind, they heard a commotion outside. It sounded like more people had arrived. They trembled as they wondered what was in store for them now.

A new face peered at the door, then left.

A while later, several people entered. They forced the people to get on their feet and go outside. They were leaving again. Who were these people and what was going to happen to them? They were still too tired and weak to protest, so they walked on.

As they left the town, they saw a pile of furs laying on a table, more furs than last time. The realization settled in. Their captors had sold them!

They were slaves.

Chapter 9

At least they now had food, a bed, and some sense of belonging. They would survive.

These new people lived differently from what they had known. Living in a permanent location, they did not forage from the forest. Instead, they grew their food in large, cleared fields.

They were needed as extra help to do the tedious work of clearing more fields, taken away from the forest, breaking up the soil for planting crops. It was heavy work, but more so because it was unfamiliar. Their bodies did not know this work and so resisted... for a while.

Others lived on this farm as well. Together, they worked the land. They, too, were here against their will. They felt powerless to do anything. Some had run away, but they always came back. The fear in their minds was, where could they go? They found themselves in an invisible prison.

The people who kept them treated them alright, that was all. They had food, very simple food. It was just enough to keep them from starving. They lived in long buildings with no privacy. Their captors gave them just enough blankets to keep them warm, but not comfortable.

Life was only tolerable.

They also learned there were many more people in this land that had journeyed from far away. They were still wandering with no direction. Would this be their future as well? Waiting to be captured and sold into slavery?

Their captors stripped these people of their heritage, forcing them to speak only their language, providing them only their food. Severe punishment was meted out if they resisted. At least now, they could all speak to each other and share their stories.

As time passed, each generation lived and passed on, being replaced by their descendants. They forgot who they had been. They became people with no history. Their story became how many fields they had dug and how many plants they had planted. Their spirit had died.

Hundreds of years later, history was about to change.

People who looked different arrived. They carried tools they used to force their captors to submit to them. They resisted at first. Death was quick.

In only a few years, they were all gone. They had not the strength or the tools, so they perished.

The people hoped the newcomers would treat them better. They had long lost their memories of being free. They just wanted to be treated better.

No such luck!

History just repeated itself and got worse. The newcomers did not even treat them as human. They lost all sense of who they were.

Chapter 10

S uzie cried as she learned the story of these people who had
continued their journey. They had chosen to not embrace their
heritage or their connection with Source. She cried and cried as she
learned of their plight. Losing their dignity and their heritage, losing
their sense of self and their freedom to be who they were born to be,
Suzie could not be consoled.

As she recited the story from her dream, the Wind Surfers listened
in sadness. Suzie then dreamed of the man whose face she saw in the
pool. She remembered his warning.

"I wonder if the man in the pool has something to do with these
people who have suffered so much. If they are, why do they think this
land is theirs, and that we should get off?

I do not understand. How can they believe these lands are theirs
alone in the future when they have nothing now?"

Condor then said, "Let's go see them and see if we can answer this
question. It is odd, isn't it?"

After consulting with the elders, they returned to the water. By
keeping their focus on the people in question, they soon found
themselves hundreds of years in the future, right near their target.

They wanted to observe unnoticed. They considered becoming a
part of their group but decided against it, as they did not appear to be
open to strangers. Then they thought about becoming like the people
who now held them as prisoners. That would not work either.

"I think we will have to be butterflies and just watch them from afar. It will be a while before we can even consider speaking to them. This will require us to keep our minds positive and neutral at the same time. We can't let ourselves get down about their plight, but we need to observe without interacting," said Goose.

"You! Never mind your food. Get to the field. We have a lot to do today," said the man. It was easy to see he had not gone short of breakfast today as Komico stared at him and his big belly hanging over his belt.

The man grabbed Komico by the arm and threw him out the door. This was going to be another horrible day. He knew when the man was this violent first thing in the day, he would be relentless. Komico would be his punching bag. But what could he do? He knew nothing else.

Today was the day something had to be done. Komico was done. Something inside him told him he deserved better than this. There must be a way to put this life to an end without having to die.

The thought of change festered in his mind. There was no chance in his day to even think about it. The man stayed nearby, watching him, yelling at him. Komico endured. He continued his work, clearing the stumps from the field as his heart sank.

As they sat together eating their meager dinner, Komico mumbled to his parents. "I do not want to work in these fields anymore. I want to have my own life. I want to leave."

His mother grabbed him, pulling him tight. "Komico, let go of ideas like that. Our destiny is here. There is no other life. If you choose to leave here, you will die. Is that what you want?"

Then his father said, "You forget those thoughts and focus on clearing the fields. He knows what you are thinking. That is why he is so hard on you. If you should do something foolish like run away, he will punish us. Is that what you want? Do you want us to take your punishment?"

Komico turned back to his dinner.

Many years passed. Komico still toiled each day in the fields. If there were no stumps to pull, there were rocks to pick. They never gave him another job. The only difference now was his children worked beside him. They were just small, but the plantation owner's son was even more brutal than his father had been. Komico could not believe that things had gotten even worse as he watched his toddlers struggle to keep up.

He could see the restlessness in his children. They wanted more. He knew if they did not have this resistance quashed, there would be trouble. As he watched them, he swallowed. It was time.

After the day's work was done, he took his children to sit beside a small creek. As they looked into the water, they saw a face appear in the water. The man smiled as he saw them.

He spoke. "There is trouble in your thoughts. You must pay heed to the outcome you desire. If you choose to make a change, it would be best if everyone makes it together. It will not be easy. Many may perish, but your decision will change your destiny if you choose to embrace it.

Find peace in yourself first. Then decide."

One day, not long after the man had spoken, they loaded Komico and a few others into a wagon. They traveled for several hours, arriving in a small town. It was a port.

Their job this day was to load boxes from a warehouse at a dock into other wagons. The men watched closely to ensure no one looked inside the boxes or ran away.

Komico's heart exploded in excitement. Maybe there is a way to escape. Not now, but soon. Komico knew he was smart enough to figure out how his new knowledge could be important to his plan.

"Now is our chance to help them," laughed Goose. "We have watched them for long enough."

"Maybe the man in the pool can help us," said Condor.

When Komico returned to the stream with his children that night, the man in the pool was there. He said, "Trust your inner voice. The time is near." He then faded away.

Komico pondered his message but did not understand. Life continued as always except for the restlessness he felt was almost unbearable.

For many days, Komico returned to the stream in the evening, hoping the man would speak. He did not.

Then he did. "There are others, new others. Trust them, for they have come to help."

The Wind Surfers knew this was their cue. However, they knew they could not just march into their lives like a marching band. This would have to be done with discretion.

"Maybe if I get his attention, you can get into his mind, Suzie." Papi was ready to go into action.

"Yes," Suzie said. "If I lead him by making suggestions, we might get them out of here."

Papi was already in butterfly before Suzie had even finished the sentence. In another minute, her mission was done.

Komico laughed as he saw the butterfly land on his arm. He held his arm out so his children could enjoy the beautiful creature that had joined them.

"Look at our visitor, my children," he said.

"Why is a butterfly sitting on your arm, daddy?" asked one of his children.

Komico just sat in the moment, enjoying it.

Suzie seized that moment to enter his mind, visualizing them sitting in a room, chatting. At first, Komico resisted, but then he recalled what the man in the pool had said. He relaxed.

"We have come to help. You must follow our instructions. There are several of us who will guide and assist you. You might not understand now, but trust us so you can be free. You must continue your life as usual until we have arranged what we need."

Chapter 11

Several nights later, the captors and their neighbors were celebrating. They were enjoying a gala dinner. They had gathered at a neighbor's home. It is a good thing everyone was there. There was music, kids screaming in pleasure as they played games, competing with the grownups talking.

It was the perfect time for action.

"Go to the barn and get the wagons ready. Do this fast, so we can get everyone out of here right away," Suzie told Komico.

He was ready! He had prepared several people his age ahead of time for this event. It had taken much persuasion, but at last, they relented. Being a slave, risk was not something that occurred often in their lives. This was the biggest risk any of them had ever taken.

An hour later, the caravan was on the road.

"Keep quiet, children. We need not attract attention," a woman said as she pulled her children into her.

They needed to hurry. If the captors discovered their absence too soon, it could bring a terrible end to their plan.

After a few nervous hours, they reached the port.

"What do we do now, Komico? We don't know anyone here. I don't know about the rest of you, but I am feeling hungry and tired," grumbled one of the older men.

"Let's sit here for a bit. The voice told me to trust, so that is what we are going to do," he replied. At that, Komico entered the silence to wait.

They saw a person walking toward them. At first, they were nervous because he did not look like them. They sat still and waited for him to make his move.

It was Goose!

He looked at Komico and said, "Pull the wagons into that warehouse over there. We need to hide them to give us more time to make a clean escape. Once that is done, I will lead you on the next step of your journey. Please stay in trust. Anyone resisting could upset the plan."

A higher level of fear creeped into the minds of these folks, trusting an outsider. However, they did as instructed. Soon they found themselves loaded on a boat, heading to open water.

"You can relax now, my friends In only a few hours, you will be free from your past," Goose told them.

"This is easy for you to say, good sir. We have never even ridden in a wagon like this before. Until only a short while ago, we had never seen this big water. It is very unsettling to be here. We were told by the voice to trust you. I hope you can see, it is just not easy," Komico said as the other grumbled in agreement.

"There is the shore we are looking for, and the end of the first leg of our journey," Goose told the group.

"We will unload here. My friends have arranged everything to make sure of your safety. We have a wonderful surprise for you when you are ashore."

And sure enough, when they arrived at the beach, Suzie and the Wind Surfers were waiting for them. They had an enormous bonfire burning to welcome them. As they beached, they tried to rush off the boat but found walking difficult. What else could they expect? This was the first time they had ever been on a boat. Their legs felt as if they were made of rubber.

Condor realized their plight as he watched, so he sent each of them a huge dose of healing energy. That did it! In only a couple of minutes, everyone had huddled around the fire. Now was Goose's favorite time. The food arrived!

As they ate and celebrated their freedom, no one noticed as the boat floated away. In a few hours, the townspeople would find it tied back up at its berth. No one the wiser.

Everyone at the party back on the farm ran inside as torrential rains poured from the skies. No one thought it unusual for it to rain hard in this season, but no one could remember it ever raining so hard. It was like the sky had fallen apart. They were thankful it only lasted about fifteen minutes.

In the morning, the ground was a mess. Fortune was on the side of our friends, so was the plight of the partiers. They were so hungover; the day was awash. It would be a day for the slaves to have to themselves.

They had not invited one fellow in the town to the party. He was not very popular amongst the locals. He was a greedy person who would do anything to cheat another from a penny.

As fortunes go, he happened to own the building where Goose had our friends stow the wagons. Well! Guess what he found in the morning? Did he report his findings? He was a happy camper!

This man knew a man in a town not far away that sold farm equipment. Six wagons would fetch a pretty penny. In the dew of early morning, the last trace of our friends disappeared down a mucky road.

"What the heck!" the farmer exclaimed as he stared into the empty room. "Have they all gone to work already?" He was feeling victorious that he had bullied these people long enough that they often went to the fields on their own.

His feelings of victory lasted as long as the road to the fields. They were not there either. He soon appeared at the door of his father's home.

"What do you mean, they have disappeared? People don't just disappear, son. Let's have another look around," the father said.

A while later, they returned to the father's home where neighbors joined them. The news had spread like wildfire. Everyone was feeling nervous, not knowing the specifics of the slaves' disappearance, or more likely, about the state of their own slaves. They wanted answers.

"We searched up and down the roads looking for clues. There was no point talking to anyone, as everyone was at our party. We ventured into the forest a few times, but everything seemed normal," the son said to the group.

As they scratched their heads, trying to figure out the next step, another son ran into the room.

"All six of our wagons are gone! The barn is empty. Many of our tools are gone as well. I looked around, trying to see if I could find any tracks, but that heavy rain last night washed everything away."

They searched again and again, up and down the roads. There were no clues! They never thought to spread their search into the town, but then, even if they had, the man who owned the warehouse was not one to tell.

It took a long time, but they accepted the slaves, and the wagons were gone.

Goose smiled as he observed how the Universe provided. Everything was in place, so now they could continue their journey in peace.

Chapter 12

Komico and his group soon found themselves far away from their miserable old life. The next morning had provided a larger boat that took them to their new home, a land far away where no one else lived... for now.

Over time, many more people arrived and settled thanks to the efforts of the Wind Surfers and Suzie. The farmers at their old home soon learned how to work the fields for themselves. There were no more slaves to be found.

They never could figure out what happened to all these people. They just disappeared every time there were those monsoon rains.

Unbeknownst to anyone else, the warehouse owner was becoming very rich!

The Wind Surfers knew they had only completed the first step in helping these people. Now the real work had to begin. This was time for a word with Rachel.

"One can only be free if they are free in their mind. These people have lived for many generations in total captivity. True freedom is foreign to them.

For them to move into the next phase, they will have to learn and accept the concept of freedom.

For these people to embrace freedom in their lives, they will have to learn how to restructure their very lives in the mundane world. We could swoosh away this problem, but it would just rise again. They must begin at the start."

The group meditated on this situation. How does one retrain a mind to accept what should be the basis of their own thinking?

Goose spoke to the group.

"We will provide you with the basic necessities for starting your new life. You need to accept that this is your life, and you need to make the choices that will determine the outcome of this new life.

Be mindful of these choices, as the ego only knows the old patterns. It will try very hard to stay in its comfort zone by recreating your old life. It has been many generations since your people knew true freedom. That path was fraught with uncertainty and danger. In fact, it led to your eventual lives as slaves.

By working together, you can reset your minds. Choose to make decisions that serve everyone's best, and you will create a new mindset.

First on the agenda, we are going to teach you how to meditate, and work with your mind. This will be the start of your renaissance. It will take everyone's participation and diligence. As each generation evolves, it will become easier. It will just be for future generations... if you do your work now.

So now it is time for you to get yourself in a comfortable position. Close your eyes and follow me in this process.

Take slow and deep breaths, moving your tummy muscles in each breath. Focus on your breath, letting your mind relax so your thoughts melt away.

Let go of the emotion evoked as the ego tries to stay in control. Do this by seeing a beautiful sun above you. The sun's rays melt the emotions into steam, so they float away into the sky. As the emotions rise, let the sun's rays soak into your being.

Relax and let yourself just be. Keep following your breath, enjoying the ongoing rhythm. Let your mind become empty except for the wonderful feeling of being one with the sun.

Stay with this visualization for as long as you can.

"How was that?" Goose asked as he saw eyes rejoining the outer world.

They sat there and smiled with a calm look on their faces. Their new life had begun.

"As you go on with your life, I ask you to use this technique every time your mind gets tangled up in old thoughts that have gotten you stuck. You are free people now. You must accept your freedom in your mind and live in this glorious concept."

It was no cakewalk to make this change of mindset. It would take many more lessons for Komico and his large family to become free. At this moment, this was enough of a lesson. Other issues were pressing on their new lives that demanded attention; such as food and lodging.

Complacency was the biggest issue to overcome. They had lived their lives by rote for so many generations. No one took risks. No one learned anything more than what was necessary for their survival.

In this new life, complacency could lead to certain death if it continued to hold their minds prisoner. Its sister, procrastination, egged it on. Never having felt any urgency to do anything for themselves, it was easy to continue in this vein. Besides, it was a beautiful spring day, so why not lie about, and relax?

They adopted the visualization Goose had taught them into their everyday lives. In fact, they did it so often that it became an excuse to procrastinate. This was not boding well.

Goose called the Wind Surfers together for a meeting. "I am not happy with the current outcome. These people are just not getting it.

There is not much change from their old mindset. If they continue like this, they will perish."

As they discussed the matter, the skies got very cloudy. Soon the skies over the people were very dark. It seemed as if nightfall had arrived early.

Rachel appeared overhead as she sent a flash of lightning through the skies. The lightning ripped open the clouds. The rain fell in sheets.

Komico and his people ran for cover in the forest. As they huddled together between the trees, they realized if they were going to survive, they needed to get busy and build some shelters.

Heavy rain continued for days. As they stood under the trees, the water rose around them. Trees started falling to the ground as the water tore away the soil from around their roots. The ground became a soggy mess. They watched their world being washed away.

After the rain stopped and the sun came out, there were many drowned rats, so to speak, as they emerged from the forest. They understood time to procrastinate was no more. No more time to be idle waiting for handouts. This life of doing nothing was over, unless they wanted to perish.

A new event occurred in their lives as they each fell to their knees. They prayed.

Not knowing who they were praying to, but if they had learned anything from this rain storm, there had to be a greater power. They had survived, so they prayed.

They asked for help. They wanted to survive. They wanted to live. Rachel smiled.

As they opened their eyes once more, they found themselves kneeling before Suzie (in the form of Merle) and the Wind Surfers. Help had arrived once more.

"This was no job for a cute little five-year-old girl," Merle thought as she took charge. Suzie could come out to play again later.

"Now that you have found motivation, it is time to make things happen. We will help you with the organizing, but you have to do the work. It is part of your retraining. Learning to fend for yourself is part of the path to finding your true freedom.

Right now, we have two issues needing our attention. Food and shelter are going to be your focus until you have achieved a satisfactory level of progress. Please choose amongst yourselves three groups of people. The first group will build shelters while the other two will focus on gathering and cooking food.

One group will forage the lands for berries and other edible plants. The other will learn to hunt for animals that will give up their lives so you can survive."

"We are ready now, Merle. What do we do? We know nothing of gathering, hunting, or building shelters," Komico said. Everyone in the group looked anxious as they stood waiting in their groups.

"Let's do our visualization again before we start. I want you to connect with the energy of this area. You need to build a relationship with the earth and its bounty. In doing so, it will provide for you."

As they repeated the meditation, they felt their energies expand. They let their energies flow into the earth, then reach high into the sky. As their breaths deepened, they expanded the energies to connect with the earth, the trees, the animals, and the plants.

When they opened their eyes, they smiled. They knew what to do. As an added bonus, more help had arrived. Standing beside Merle was Klum.

"I have come to aid you in knowing the plant world. For your survival, you need to become intimate with our friends, the plants. They are your first line of defense and survival in this wonderful world. Those of you who will forage will work with me.

Plants are living creatures, just like us. In that, we need to treat them with respect. We need to know their purpose so we can use them as designed. Misusing them can have undesirable results.

The first step in building relationships with plants is learning how to differentiate between each one."

Klum walked with his wildcrafting group. First, they walked in the meadows. He taught them how to see plants. They learned plants are far more than just green things or pretty flowers.

It was not long before their medicine baskets were full, and they knew how to use the plants correctly. Their food baskets were also full.

"Always remember to give thanks as you pick the plants. Ask the plant if it is willing to give its life for you. If it does, the plant will separate with no resistance. If not, then leave it alone and say thank you," Klum said as they entered the forest.

"Plants from the forest differ from their friends, the meadow plants. They get less sunlight than their meadow cousins. This means their nutrition is in a different part of the plant. They are more often hanging on bushes like berries or found under the ground, or even growing on the side of a tree. Let's find some examples.

Here are some yummy salmonberries. They grow on bushes. So do these huckleberries. If we go deeper into the forest, we can dig into the earth and find mushrooms. Be careful though, many mushrooms and their cousins, the toadstools are poisonous. They can make a person awful sick."

The people were getting excited. This was a great starting place for their re-education. After all, who doesn't love to eat?

Another of Rachel's friends by the name of Grey Eagle joined in the fun. His job was to teach people how to hunt.

Grey Eagle stood in front of his group. They were keen to learn to hunt, but did not know how to do so. They did not even have knives suitable for making bows and arrows. This was going to be a beginner's course!

Before the session began, e had scoured the area in search of the right rocks for making knives. They were fortunate again that there was a flint outcropping not far away from their camp. He took the members to the site, then showed them how to break the rock and to work pieces of the flint into the shape of knives.

"Now, once we have the knife ready, the next step is to find the right bushes for making arrows and tree branches for making bows. We may have to go deeper into the forest to find the right vines for the bowstrings," he said.

It took a long time to find the required material for making the bows, but it did happen. They also found good branches for making spears. With the vines that were picked for making bows, they learned a second use; how to make traps for small animals.

The third group fell to the Wind Surfers. None of these people had ever built a shelter before, but then, there was not much they could not do if they set their mind to it! We have seen much evidence in prior stories, right?

"I think if this is going to be a permanent home for them, this mud would be a good possibility," suggested Raven.

"It is pretty mucky clay, so maybe we can form it into bricks and bake them. That way, they will build houses that can stand differing temperatures over the seasons," added Condor.

They got the group split into various task groups. One group dug a burning pit for baking the bricks. Another group made forms and started filling them with mud.

As the group dug the baking pit, Grey Eagle approached. "That pit looks just right for baking animals as well. Let's dig a second one over in the cooking area and get a fire going in it. Then we can roast whatever we bring back from our hunt today. I think everyone will enjoy a splendid feast of roast meat after we are done for the day."

The people working on the brick pit just smiled at Grey Eagle and nodded as they looked forward to some wonderful success. With any luck, there would be a fabulous meal coming up.

Merle and Goose stood together, watching the hubbub of activity around them. They could see the shift in their friends' energies as new feelings of self-motivation and self-responsibility integrated into their minds. They seemed so much lighter and happier as they carried out the labors of the day.

Secretly, Rachel worked quietly overhead, speaking uplifting words into their minds.

"Now that you have begun to understand the value of working to look after yourself, I am going to help you clear some of the old trauma you have suffered. This does not mean you will not have to do any clearing yourself. It will just make it easier."

At that, she created a gentle breeze that swished through the land, such a little breeze that none of the people even noticed it. But it did its job. Many years passed before these people would realize how the painful memories of the suffering of their ancestors, the little breeze released and returned to the Universe that day.

They did notice they felt more relaxed, and it was easier to walk and work as they carried out their tasks. It was not very long before they heard singing and whistling from their friends as they worked. They did not even realize this was happening because it seemed so natural. That they had not even felt happy enough to whistle or sing for hundreds of years did not enter their minds.

There was a group of very proud people sitting on clouds above the village, as they watched their trainees find themselves and build a new history for their people.

Chapter 13

I t was a wonderful day to celebrate! The last building was done, and the family units had moved in.

It had taken several months to build enough houses. In fact, since they were used to living communally anyway, they built longhouses for the families to share rather than having each family unit living in their own little home. That saved a lot of time!

Did someone say celebrate?

The Wind Surfers met to discuss how they could help to make this day a memorable event.

"I do not think it will work well if we just manifest flutes and other future instruments so we can party with these people. They may have accepted us and know we have unusual skills, but it might be better if we stay with the age we are in," said Condor.

Poor Hummingbird! He had not blasted off in a fit of ecstasy for so long. He was hoping today was the day. As he accepted his fate, a brilliant idea floated into his mind!

"How about if I go into the forest and get some birds to celebrate with us? If we have lots of them singing and flying about, no one will notice I am not here!"

Everyone cheered as Hummingbird set off with Songbird right at his side.

"You are not going anywhere without me, my friend! I need this too!"

They wanted to play music but did not know how to do so in this period since flutes and guitars had not been invented yet. They meditated on the problem.

As they sat in the quiet, Rachel showed them how to make drums using sticks and hollow logs. Tonight would be a real party!

And so it was. As they removed the roast deer and potatoes from the in-ground oven, everyone was ready to celebrate.

As the celebration unfolded, everyone closed their eyes, connecting with Source to give thanks to the plants and animals that had made this meal possible.

Opening their eyes, they gave an enormous spontaneous cheer. They were all so happy. They had accomplished so much.

The dinner was delicious! Satisfied smiles abounded on the faces of these folks!

Meal done; the music began. The six remaining Wind Surfers sat facing a big old cottonwood log, hollowed out by time. They had fashioned drum sticks from branches. Now they were ready to play... and they did!

At the first beat of the drum, the skies filled with the sweet chirps of hundreds of songbirds nestled in the trees. One could imagine no finer music.

Now that everyone had a home, they could relax. It is amazing how much having a home made a difference to their mindset. To the Wind Surfers, their happy smiles were full payment for their efforts.

But was their job done here?

One might think so, but even though these people had released themselves from their traumatic pasts, and now shared lovely homes together, the Wind Surfers knew the bigger challenges still lie ahead.

A few days after the celebrations were done, they sat together in their virtual room. With big frowns on their faces, they viewed the little community from above.

"We may have moved them from that terrible situation, but they have not removed themselves from that lifestyle," said Suzie.

"Yes, they are acting as if they are still slaves. They are showing no independent initiative. As long as we gave them direction, they did the work. Now that this project is complete, they are just sitting around the campfires. They are not even meditating," said Condor.

"It looks as if they are waiting for more instructions. So I guess the next job we have is to teach them how to instruct themselves," laughed Goose.

Suzie headed down and spoke to the people.

"To complete the mission of moving past your past, you each must learn to create your own destiny.

One of the first challenges to move past is your belief that you are a slave. If you cannot move past the slave mentality, you will always see yourself as needing permission from others before you take any action.

Please get comfy and close your eyes so I can lead you in a visualization to help you reframe your beliefs about authority.

Allow yourselves to see yourself as you looked as a young child. By allowing your inner child to learn and accept its own power, the adult within you will also learn to accept its own power.

See yourself standing beside your parents. Can you see how much difference in height are you to your mom? And your father?

How do you feel as this child standing by your parents?

Do you feel smaller? Do you feel less powerful?

Sit in this picture for a few minutes, letting yourself be in the situation.

Take a deep breath, hold, slowly breathing out.

Pull yourself up to the height of your mother. Take a deep breath and smile at her. You are now equals in power.

Take another deep breath. Raise yourself and your mother to the height of your father.

One more deep breath, and smile at your father. You are all now the same height.

A last deep breath. Embrace the feeling of being fully in your own power.

If you feel uncomfortable in this feeling, take a deep breath and see those old, limited feelings releasing and flying away from your being.

Relax. Take another deep breath and find your quiet place.

Repeat this exercise for as many days as you need until you embrace your full power. By supporting yourself as an equal to, and as empowered as your parents, you are giving yourself permission to live your life as you choose. The beliefs about your own lack of empowerment fade away with each thought that leaves your mind. You are in charge of your mind, your beliefs, and your life. You are a fully empowered person.

Give thanks to the Cosmic for helping you release your mindset so you can create this wonderful new life.

As you give thanks, let your mind wander so it can show you how to move forward into this new life. It is yours. You just let go and take action. Your new life is here."

Suzie closed off the visualization by returning to the clouds. She left them to meditate on their own.

Chapter 14

At Greenwood Commons, life carried on. The residents were now accustomed to the people living at their front gate. They still brought them food and whatever else they needed for them for comfort, but they were still there.

They did not try to do anything but sit.

The Wind Surfers, and their leader Suzie, had jumped forward in time to see how the situation was progressing.

"Well, it is a start," said Goose.

"We still need to work in the past to change their history some more. These people need to find their own personal power and their destiny," said Suzie. "There has to be more we can do."

And with that, all nine headed back in time.

———————————

Many years had passed since leaving these folks to determine their own fate. In fact, it had been so long that the memories of Suzie and the Wind Surfers had become legends. Most of the residents did not even believe these people had even existed for real.

They were now just stories around the campfire.

"Before we interact with them, let's observe what their lives are like so we can see what is working and what is not," Suzie said as they arrived.

Since time was not an issue, the group observed them for several weeks. They wanted to see how they interacted, how they supported themselves in their daily lives, and how they observed their relationship with the Cosmic.

It was obvious they had learned to look after themselves. They had become very handy at working the land. Klum had stayed with them for many years, ensuring their knowledge of the local plant life was well embedded in their minds. He also made sure their farming practices supported the land. All was well from his perspective.

Grey Eagle had taught them to be skilled hunters. Everyone rejoiced in the bounty. They thrived. They always gave thanks to the plants and animals for providing to them and for giving their lives.

"Everyone seems to be doing so well," Condor said, scratching his head. "It is a mystery why the people in the future are still sitting in front of Greenwood Commons. There must be something missing."

It took a few more weeks of observation until the light came on.

"I think I have it! Said Goose. "They have gone back to sleep again. They have no challenge in their lives, so they are just doing things by habit."

"You are right!" exclaimed Suzie. "Even when they pray, they make offers to the Cosmic and to the animals, but they are by rote. There is no feeling in them."

"How can we shake them up to bring them back to life again?" asked Raven.

As fast as Raven asked, the sky became very cloudy and ominous. A storm was brewing. There would be a big shakeup tonight. As they looked up into the sky, they saw Rachel wink at them. She knew what to do.

The rain fell. Not a gentle rain like the people were used to, but a harsh, wind-driven rain. They ran for their homes as fear filled their minds.

The storm lasted for days. It crushed their crops, flooding the fields.

It was so wet they could not even go outside to hunt or even to get firewood. All they could do was sit in their homes, watching the fires die as their food and wood ran out.

It seemed the rain had destroyed the life they had known. Hopelessness and anger set in.

All they had worked for was gone. Now what?

The storm was relentless. It just continued like the end of the world was near. Water had even crept into the longhouses. Would this be the end of this little community?

"Maybe we need to pray for help," suggested a little girl. "Maybe the Cosmic is trying to tell us something."

"Hush my daughter. You are not old enough to know anything yet. We do our prayers every day. We even have them written, so we say them correctly," said her mother.

"But maybe we need to say them better," she replied in a soft, almost apologetic tone.

It took the mother a while to understand what the daughter had said. When it did click, she smiled, then she laughed. A huge laugh that was so loud it shocked everyone in the building. The last thing anyone expected was the sound of joy. After all, they were busy practicing being hard done by. How could anyone find something to laugh about?

"My people, we have the answer. My little daughter, who I chastised because she is so young, is the most mature of all of us.

We might remember to do our prayers every day, but do they mean anything to us or are they just words, habits that bring comfort to us as we pass through our days?

Let us all pray to the God of our hearts. Let us pray in thanks. Let us rejoice that we have wonderful lives with peace, abundance, and good health. Let us be sincere in our prayers, letting gratitude be the driving force in our lives. Let us throw our prayer books in the garbage."

The mother sat down by the now extinguished fire, taking her daughter's hand in hers. As she prayed, she felt her husband take her other hand.

People moved closer, forming a tight circle. They held each other's hands as they prayed. They let themselves feel the gratitude that had festered inside them, unrecognized from years of living by habit. The gratitude blossomed.

Soon, they could feel their connection expand. Feelings of safety returned. This situation would end well. Lessons learned. They knew their own stagnant thinking had created it. Through their prayers, they remembered... and reconnected with the Cosmic.

Prayers done. Opening their eyes, they rose and stepped outside. To their amazement, the land was as they had left it before the storm.

They gazed at their gardens, full of ripening vegetables. The fruit on their trees hung low, ripened and ready to pick, glistened in the sun.

The people smiled, and once again gave thanks.

Rachel winked again as the Wind Surfers and Suzie watched. Was this the conclusive answer to the situation at Greenwood Commons?

They knew deep inside this lesson had helped get these people back on track. The people at Greenwood Commons needed to be conscious of their relationship with the Universe. For now, these folks would never take their relationship with the Cosmic for granted again. Hopefully, it would be paid forward.

"Well, we can strike that problem off the list, but we still are not there yet," Suzie announced.

"They are still living their lives by habit. It works well for them, so they do not need to expand their knowledge outside of this little bubble," said Goose.

"Last time Songbird and I went for a fun flight, we traveled many miles, but we stayed in this time. We saw another village over those mountains. We never thought twice about mentioning it because we knew the focus was on these people," said Hummingbird.

"That's it!" shouted Suzie, laughing with glee. "They need some new neighbors!"

It was time to go hunting again. The animals, often close by, had gone away. Hunting was no longer a dash into the woods. They were going to have to travel further.

They were feeling uncomfortable with this change. Preparing for overnight camping or cooking away from their home fire was unfamiliar territory. For a few moments, they even regretted having chosen to be the hunters. They thought the job brought them glory. They did not plan to work too.

"We need to buck up and get this done, fellows, so let's do our prayers and get moving," the leader of the hunting group said.

They all sat down and prayed, asking the Cosmic to provide well for their people and to keep them safe. Once done, off they went.

It was not long before the grumbling started. It seemed obvious the Cosmic was not listening. They foraged all day, surviving on plants alone. Not even a rabbit. Faces were so long they almost tripped on them when they set up camp that evening.

They had chosen a beautiful little spot right beside a lake. It was an unfamiliar scene for them. They did not even know of such things as lakes. Big waters existed only in legends. Not sure if this might be one, it made little sense because they could see trees on the other side. They were very far away, but they were trees over there.

As they sat resting, they watched the lake. It fascinated them. They watched a huge eagle swooped out of the sky. It screeched down into the surface of the lake, rising out of the water with something in its talons. They watched it as it flew to a nearby tree with its prize.

Staring at the developing scene, hypnotized by the event, a fish jumped out of the water. They looked at each other in wonder as it splashed its way back in. They did not know of fish or fishing. Another fish jumped. Another eagle swooped.

"The eagles are eating those things jumping out of the water!" one fellow exclaimed. "I wonder if this is a sign for us to do the same."

"How can we get to them, though? We have already tried walking on this water. All we got was wet. We have never seen this much water in one place. The food, if that is what it is, is too far out."

With that, they turned away from the entertainment on the lake. They prepared to sleep.

During the night, they dreamed. They dreamed of eating these animals in the water. They felt their bellies full and happy.

In the morning, rather than returning home, they decided to take a day off from hunting so they could figure out the message in their dreams.

Being a restless bunch, they opted to hike along the edge of the lake. They felt very nervous. They did not know what to expect. Not knowing how far they might have to walk, they agreed to the journey for as long as they felt comfortable. They would then turn back to their camp.

The only notable event in the walk was crossing a fast-moving stream. There were no streams like this in their land, so, again, they had to figure out how to solve this new challenge. How were they to continue their journey with this enormous obstacle in the way?

Some thought this was a sign to turn back, but their leader said, "We must look to see if we can find a way to get over this river. Let's be brave and face this challenge in trust."

They walked up the stream a fair way, looking for a clue. Luck was with them as they saw a large tree lying right across the stream, just around a bend. The creek was shallow at this point. Holding onto the fallen tree provided them with a good handhold to cross.

As they pushed through this obstacle, one man jumped back, almost losing his footing as a startled fish splashed about nearby. They all stopped and stared.

"If those are the same animals as the eagles were catching in their talons, then maybe we can catch some here," he said.

Sitting at the far edge of the creek, they watched the stream. Several fish lazed about in small pools with not a care in the world. One man jumped up and ran into the pool. He reached into the water, attempting to catch a fish. The fish eluded him. In fact, he had scared all the fish nearby. The pool was now empty.

Returning to his seat with the others. He pondered.

As he meditated on the problem, he began thinking about how they used to catch deer. He realized they might adapt the idea for catching the fish.

He headed into the bush nearby. There were willow hummocks nearby, so he cut some twigs, making them long enough to block the exit from the pool.

It had taken long enough to cut the twigs that the fish had returned. The man surveyed the pool, determining the entrance and exit. He then pushed the long twigs deep into the streambed at each end until they formed a pen. The fish could not escape.

It was fascinating to watch as he worked. Once he was done, the others patted him on the back, then stared again at the pool. Now how were they going to get their hands on these fish? Even if they were now captive, they were still going to be a tough catch. Slippery little beasts they were.

One fellow jumped in, trying to catch one in his bare hands. All he got was wet.

Another one, thinking again of how they would deal with the situation if it was a deer, picked up his bow and arrow. He shot an arrow straight into the water, missing by only an inch.

He tried again and again but kept missing. (They had not taught them about refraction in school, I guess!)

In desperation, he walked right into the pool. He stood over the fish (creating shade), then shot. He hit his target!

With the fish on shore, they gave thanks to the Cosmic, both for the food and for the answer.

Several of the men set to building a fire while others grabbed their bows to catch more fish. They were starving since all they had subsisted on was wild plants for almost two days.

Even though the eagle had eaten his fish raw, they felt cooking the fish would be the right thing to do since they ate no other meat raw.

When they relaxed and kept their minds open, their inner guidance showed them how to cook the fish.

As the fire burned down, they cut some long willow hummocks, leaving a nub of a branch near the top. Placing them at either side of the fire, they skewered the gutted fish onto a long branch. With the branch resting between the branches, the fish now dangled high over the hot coals.

Now they were getting excited! Their tummies longed for solid food.

Before they ate the fish, they placed the entrails and other leftover parts in a pile away from their camp, hoping some wild animal would benefit. They gave thanks to the Cosmic for providing both the lesson and for the food.

That night, another dream came to them. They realized they had taken another step toward owning their power. Feeling like fulfilled people, they knew they had achieved something special that day. Happy campers were they.

Now, being able to fend for themselves on the trail, they felt more comfortable being on this journey. However, they soon recalled the reason for their trip; people at home were hungry.

Fashioning crude baskets from willow hummocks, the men filled them with as many fish as they could catch. They knew they would have to hurry to get them home so they would not spoil.

This proved to be a fruitless task. As they worked through the return trip, they could smell the fish emitting an unpleasant odor.

"I think the fish are going bad," one of them said as they stopped to make a meal.

"We had better cook them all now or there will be nothing to give to the others when we get home. We are going to either have to find a closer source or figure out how to preserve this food for future trips," another said.

As the fish cooked, they meditated. They saw a vision showing them how to cure the fish by smoking them.

When they opened their eyes, they followed the guidance of the visualization, setting the fire so it created a lot of hot smoke. They cut the fish into strips, then hung them on branches over the smoky pit.

It took a long time for the fish to cook this way, so several of the men headed off into the forest in search of other food. From far away, Klum guided the men to the right spots as Morel mushrooms fell into their hands from beneath the tree roots. Their packs would be full of all kinds of yummy goodies by the time they returned home.

The men realized they had now found a new viable food source.

They also realized they had developed a yearning for adventure. The little voice in their minds asked them what was beyond the lake?

It was time for them to return home first, but a new chapter in their lives was unfolding.

Chapter 15

Venturing further into the forest was all the men had on their minds once they had arrived home. Their surprise for their families paled in comparison. It was not long before their shoes were heading off again. Several other people who were not hunters joined them this time. After all, enthusiasm is contagious!

It seemed like just a short hop back to the lake. The new members stared at the big water in disbelief. They had never dreamed of such a wondrous sight. And when a fish jumped, it was almost too much. Any trepidation about joining in on this adventure had now vaporized!

A quick meal of fish caught right out of a stream, and they were back on the trail. One could almost see a cloud of dust from the enthusiasm driving their feet.

It did not take long after circling the lake for the terrain to begin its rise. It started as a gradual climb, but that changed in only a short distance as the angle of the land became steeper. There were no defined trails to follow, so they took their time. Every so often, they stopped to rest and meditate. They wanted guidance.

Everything felt good, so they continued; slow but sure. As they walked, they noticed that the plants around them were unfamiliar. Even the trees were shorter than the hikers.

It had taken most of the day, but they did find the top. However, it was not a case of just pop over the top and sliding down.

No, the top was visible, and they could look right over it. But, at first glance to these novice eyes, it seemed this might be as far as they would get.

Boy! Where were the Wind Surfers and their climbing equipment? Somewhere in the future, I bet! The Wind Surfers had been watching them from far above, sitting on their cloud. They knew this was not a mission for them to interfere in. These people needed to figure it out themselves, so no harnesses today!

Late in the day, they searched for a flat spot to camp. It was right beside a lovely little waterfall. They guzzled the sparkling water, smiling with satisfaction, as they looked back to the lowlands from where they had come. It was breathtaking.

"There has to be a break in the top that will let us cross this barrier. We have come this far; we need to succeed. I feel there is something for us on the other side," one hunter said as they pondered their situation.

After they had rested for a while, having enjoyed a delicious dinner of wild plants and some rabbits who had offered themselves up, this same person rose to his feet. He looked at the others.

"My senses tell me there is a way to get over the mountain and we are near it. I am going to take a walk to scout this area out to see if I am right. If anyone cares to join me, let's go."

With that, a small group headed off on a new adventure. They followed the little waterfall up as far as they could. Somehow they felt it would widen out, creating a pass.

They were right. It only took them about a half hour. Finding themselves looking at a brand new world where they could safely stand to see what lay before them. Now, they were getting excited!

They stood for quite a long time when it appeared before them. It was smoke! Not a forest fire, but a cluster of campfire smoke, way off in the distance. They gulped as they recognized it. There must be others!

Arriving back at the camp, they blurted out the news.

"Never mind getting over the top! There are others! We saw smoke from a village!" they yelled.

"We need to meditate on this matter. It would be best for us to understand what this means. We have never met others. For as far back as our history goes, we have been the only ones. Now we know we are not," said the leader.

As they meditated, they passed into sleep. Dreamworld was very busy this night. There were questions to be answered. They could not deny these questions. Even if they turned back now and went home, they would still know they were no longer alone.

In the morning, concern still showed on their faces over this life-shaking revelation. They were feeling nervous about what to do. Their dreams had not answered their questions.

As they sat with their breakfast, they remained quiet. They all knew that going forward into uncertainty was their only choice. But what was in that future? Who was at this camp?

"Maybe I can help bring peace to your minds," she said, smiling at the folks gathered around their fire.

One would have thought they were hearing a clap of thunder. Hearing her voice, they clung to each other as shock took control of their minds. It took a couple of minutes for them to sort themselves out again when they realized there was no danger.

"My name is Portu. I come from the village of the smoke. Since you can see our village, it is my privilege to welcome you. Only those who have evolved to a high enough spiritual level can see our village."

They still sat with their mouths hanging wide open. They could not speak a word in reply.

Where had this little lady come from? She did not look like she had hiked for days like they did. She looked as fresh as the morning they now enjoyed.

"I suggest you take some time to meditate on this situation. Your minds cannot seem to accept that I stand here before you in friendship," Portu said, as she sat down on a nearby log, closing her eyes.

As the men relaxed into meditation, they saw Rachel smiling down at them. They knew this was a sign.

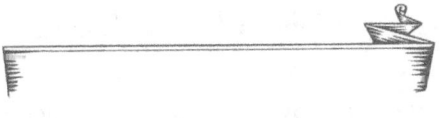

Chapter 16

T he men sat by the large center fire of the village, enjoying a cup of the most wonderful tea. The trek down the mountain seemed to take only minutes compared to the struggles of the previous days. Now they sat with the elder, not saying a thing, just enjoying the moment.

There was something familiar about these people, it seemed. This was an odd feeling because they had known no other people since they arrived in this land hundreds of years ago... but there it was, this feeling of familiarity. Somehow, they just knew these people.

As they drank their tea, they slipped into meditation. Rachel appeared before them. She looked different today. Smiling her biggest smile, she looked divine wearing a lavender gown.

"Today I introduce myself in my highest glory, as this is a most auspicious occasion. In truth, I am so much more than just your guiding angel. It is now my pleasure to provide you the opportunity to raise your consciousness to a higher and most glorious level. Allow me to introduce myself.

I am Rachel. I serve the Universal God that created this earth and all that exists. I invite you to join me in this moment of knowing yourself through the eyes of God.

Let your minds relax, for we shall go on a journey, a long journey, back in time."

As they relaxed, a soft wind blew. It seemed to lift them from their seats and carry them away. They drifted with the wind for what seemed like an eternity, seeing nothing as they traveled. All they could feel was the wind, taking them somewhere unknown.

Trusting her, they knew Rachel was guiding them. Something new, something important, was about to be revealed.

When the wind had subsided, they opened their eyes. It seemed odd to them at first. They were sitting in the same place as before the wind had carried them off!

They sat in the quiet, waiting for Rachel to reveal.

As they sat looking around, a realization came crashing down. They were in the same place, but it was a different time!

It was like they were standing at the side of the scene that was unfolding. A sizable group of people sat by the fire. They recognized the Elder who had welcomed them into their village. And there was Portu, smiling at them. Many looked very uncomfortable as they sat.

Portu's people tried their best to help them relax, but they could not. Before long, these people rose, gathered their belongings, and walked away. The love and kindness offered to them, rejected.

They felt sad for these people, watching them walk away into an unknown future.

This scene replayed itself again and again in their minds. It was trying to reveal something it wanted them to know. But what?

As the Destiny Tea took them deeper into their minds, they traveled back in time. It took them back to a vision of people enslaved by others, living desperate lives of nothingness. They felt the numbness set in as their minds protected them from the misery and trauma of the people living this hopeless life.

They traveled deeper, back to a time when they felt the pain of extreme hunger and hopelessness. A time of feeling lost.

Then came the prize!

They saw themselves sitting by the campfire again, sitting with the Elder and Portu.

The journey had left them feeling miserable and threatened. They could not, and did not want to understand what these people offered.

Looking around, they realized they were looking at their own family history. The visions had immersed them in their own karma. A karma created by the choices of their ancestors. Choices made in fear.

It became a soulful cry as their minds melted, knowing the suffering their ancestors had endured for many hundreds of years, as it played before them in their minds.

Rachel then spoke to the men in her best quiet voice.

"You have now seen how the choices of your ancestors shaped your very own lives so many generations later. Not all is lost if you choose to embrace this lesson. If you choose to forgive your family, for they made choices from a lower, less enlightened mind, you may embrace the lessons learned. You may rewrite your family history, and feel the love of the Universe, as our Beloved intended.

Rachel watched as her beloved children pondered her statements. She could feel their struggle. It was not a difficult struggle, though. After all, who would want to choose to suffer, especially when the love they so cherished was right at hand?

Opening their eyes, they breathed it in, as Rachel swished her hand above them, releasing a cloud of special dust. They glowed. Their energy fields becoming so intensified, becoming so brilliant, those who watched had to cover their eyes.

They relaxed, falling into a coma, laying on the ground. The energies of their family past released their hold, their karma drifted into the ethers.

Dave and the folks at Greenwood Commons were busy working on the new gardens for the children. Everyone was there to help. Nothing could make a day better than working with nature and sharing it with their children.

As they worked away, Suzie and all the Wind Surfers watched from above.

Projecting her most loving smile, Suzie waved at her mom and dad, having fun in the garden. She could see they did not feel sad because their daughter had gone away. They lived in the love that embraced them, knowing all was well.

But what had happened to the people at the front gate?

Had the events of their ancestors changed anything for this present day gathering?

There were still people sitting at the front gate, but what is this?

There were fewer of them. Why?

Suzie and her friends would have to check this out. Maybe they went home... or?

The people that were still sitting there were busy making crafts. They had even set up a roadside booth. People were stopping by and buying their wonderful products.

These folks hardly seemed like the earlier people that had tried to chase off the residents of Greenwood Commons. They shone like people proud of themselves, self-empowered.

As they watched the episode unfolding before them, they noticed a car parked in the shadows down the road. It had that look of a government vehicle. Wanting to know more, Papi donned her inner butterfly and fluttered over to the car.

She wanted to land right on the person inside, however, the windows were all closed, so she landed on the windshield. However, the appearance of the little butterfly frightened the woman so much that she slapped the windshield, so hard, she cracked it.

"Get out of the way, you stupid vermin! I am trying to film what is going on up the street!" she said. Papi did not light soon enough for her, so she hit the windshield again. This time, her slap destroyed the windshield.

I won't tell you what she said at this point, because it was not very polite. However, she drove away in a manner that definitely contravened the Motor Vehicle Act, soon finding herself wearing a parked car.

This would not go down as a good day for this poor government employee. Lucky for her, the movie camera was still operating, so she could use it to explain to her boss how her day went.

Chapter 17

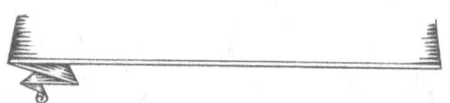

I t was many days later when the men returned to consciousness. They lay in a comfy bed in a house, covered in cozy furs. Had they died and gone to heaven?

As they opened their eyes and stirred, the villagers brought them a nourishing drink and small bits of food. This was not heaven, but it felt close enough.

It took a full day for the men to return to real life. It was a bit of a struggle. The other side was so inviting, as a good sleep always is. However, deep inside, something stirred that demanded attention. They needed to go home.

It took another full day for them to prepare, even though they had little to take for the journey. They sat by the main fire, meditating on the flames.

Later in the day, the Elder sat with them. He said, "It is your choice now whether you move on or if you choose to stay with us. If you choose to move on, you risk losing the frequency you have attained in this camp. However, it is now a frequency you are familiar with. If you have attained a high enough level of consciousness, you will find us again as you journey."

Hamrock, their leader, said in reply, "Most gracious Elder, we appreciate and give thanks for all you have provided for us during our time with you. However, we must return to enlighten our people. This level of consciousness feels natural now. Making choices from fear has caused endless suffering for our ancestors. To honor our ancestors, we choose the higher path, the path of love.

We thank Guardian Angel Rachel for clearing the trauma of our past from our memories. "

After a few minutes of prayer, the Elder rose, with Portu at his side. He looked at Hamrock and his people with a smile, like a father whose children had just graduated from high school. They too rose, then turned toward home with the first step in a brand new journey.

Chapter 18

"We were all sitting around the center fire outside. Everyone was sitting staring at the fire. It had been such a strange week. None of us knew what to do except sit in the bliss," Hamrock's wife said to him as they caught up on recent events.

Since he was a polite person, he let her speak first, so she had no awareness of the goings-on at Portu's village, or even of Portu's village.

"It was the middle of the day. We had got all of our work done earlier, so we just relaxed and enjoyed some down time. After we had been there for a while, the strangest thing happened." She struggled to keep her composure as she recollected such a strange experience.

"A group of scruffy looking men walked right through our village. There were many of them, so it took several minutes for them to cross through. They were looking for something, I do not know what... but they never saw us!" she said with a look of incredulity on her face.

"Some walked right through the fire pit but did not know it was there. Others walked right through our buildings without even slowing down. Everyone stayed quiet until these scary-looking foreigners passed through. They looked different from us, and they spoke a language we did not know.

As they walked, they seemed puzzled. Even though we could not understand their language, it was easy to tell they had expected something to be in a particular place, but it was not.

A couple of days later, we were busy doing our chores. It was around lunch, so we were cooking when they returned. We had a delicious side of deer roasting on a spit.

This time, they seemed downright angry. Whatever they were looking for was not here. They walked right through the camp again.

They continued talking and walking. We watched them as they disappeared up the path. We never saw them again. They did not even acknowledge the smell of the deer over the fire!"

Hamrock sat without saying a word for a few moments. If his wife thought that was weird, just wait until he filled her in on their experiences! He wondered if there was a connection.

The other members of Hamrock's group joined them at their fire. They brought their families. By the time they were ready to tell their story, the entire village had settled in.

Hamrock began. "After we set out the second time from bringing you the fish, we headed into the mountains. We wanted to see if we could get over them.

By traveling around the edge of the lake, we found a clearing where we could start the climb. Those are big mountains when you get up close!" he laughed.

"The climbing became quite difficult, especially since we were not used to anything but flat land, but we found our way close to the top. When we stopped for the night, Bikkram and Boljie went a bit further to see if they could find a trail over the top. It did not take long. There it was! Bikkram, tell them what you saw, my friend."

Bikkram was glad he could have time to speak. Telling stories was his favorite pastime. Hugging his wife, he stood in the center of the group with his back to the fire. He began.

"As soon as Boljie and I got a view over the top, we saw smoke. Not a forest fire, but columns of smoke like there was a village in the valley ahead. Our feet could not move fast enough. We didn't even know there were others, and here appeared a village off in the distance."

Boljie then jumped in. "That night, we all had a restless sleep. Our dreams tried to figure out what we had observed, but in the morning, we all still felt very confused."

Bikkram could not contain himself anymore, so he blurted out, "A woman came to visit us during breakfast. She just appeared!

Portu suggested she could answer our questions if we liked. As she sat down on a log, she looked like an old friend who had come for a visit."

Hamrock wanted to get his two cents in again, so he took the reins. "She invited us to her village. She told us that since we could see the smoke from her village, we had raised our consciousness high enough to be welcomed by her people."

Hamrock then turned to his wife. "Dearest one, how long ago did the men walk through the village?"

"It was the day after the second new moon. I recall it well. It had been so dark the night before."

All the people who had been with Hamrock on the journey laughed as they realized the connection.

"My dearest one, that was the first night we stayed in Portu's village. I guess because being with these people, our energy had lifted high enough that we could communicate with them. It must have raised your energy as well," Hamrock said, as the reality sank in.

"Those men were looking for us. They were slave hunters. The Elder told us all about our ancestral history. When some of our ancestors walked away from Portu's people, their energy dropped to a level that they could not look after themselves. These men you saw found them and made them slaves. They were looking for us!.. to make us slaves."

Everyone gasped in astonishment. Those who had not traveled to Portu's village started asking so many questions that the discussion fell apart.

Hamrock sat holding his wife's hand, sobbing. Reality was now setting in. The Elder had spoken the truth.

In time, everyone in the little village came to understand the truths that the Elder had told the men. They now understood why they felt different. It was a good different, so they were determined to keep it.

They rested with the new, higher energy for a long time. Meditation was more than a daily ritual now. It was a way of life. They could now speak with beings in other realms for guidance.

Soon it became time for the Wind Surfers, and don't forget our dear little Suzie, to join back in.

"There are many other villages within a reasonable walk from your home. It is time now to reach out to them to make new friends and trading partners." Suzie told the people as they sat in council.

"We have determined where many are located, but we have not tried to communicate with them, so we do not know how accepting of you they will be. This will be an opportunity for you to practice your positive living lessons.

We will watch how things develop and make suggestions as need arises. Guardian Angel Rachel is also monitoring the situation, but she will only be involved in emergencies. The bulk of the work is up to you folks. It is helping you rewrite your history.

Chapter 19

Excitement over the upcoming trip overtook the normal routine of the village. The very idea that other people were not only close by, but had been for who knows how long, became almost unbearable as daydreams of new friends lit up their dreams.

The organization committee was meeting this day. They wanted to have everything just right for the adventure into this next phase of existence, so careful planning slowed down the dream of making new friends.

As the men sat huddled by a fire one evening, several young ladies approached them. It was obvious they had something on their mind they wished to share.

"We wish to make the journey with you," stated Tampica, the eldest of the group. "Maybe we can be an enticement for their friendship. If they have the same challenges we have, being such a small community, they might have some nice boys for us to marry. That way, we can be relatives instead of just friends!"

The men sat there staring at the girls for a moment, pondering what Tampica had said. It had not occurred to them that this problem even existed, or that a viable solution might be at hand.

The traveling band just grew larger! They agreed that only a few of the girls would travel with the men since it would put too much of a strain on the others to have all of them make the journey. After all, they were important contributors to the life of the village... and life at home needed to carry on, even if everyone's focus was on the trip!

This decision delayed the trip for a couple of days. Since it was an important addition to the mission, no one minded. After all, there was an agenda, but not a fixed timeline.

The day was now at hand. It was a nice day, sunny and cool in the early morning. A perfect day for a walk, and a walk it would be!

They were very familiar with the land over the first few days, as this was their traditional hunting area. This made the walk easy. Everyone walked along at a comfortable pace, chatting, often reminiscing about the successful hunts they had enjoyed over the years as they passed landmarks that brought back floods of memories.

No one had ever questioned why they had never traveled further than this area in all the generations of hunting they had enjoyed. They had always come home with their bounty, so there had never been a necessity to venture further.

As they passed into new forests, the terrain rose. They prepared in their minds for new possibilities as they reminisced.

It was late in the day, so they set up camp for the night. Several people, including some girls, headed to have some fun catching some fish in a nearby stream while the others set up tents and made fires.

That evening, as they sat around the fire, discussions began.

Hamrock led the discussion. "We need to be looking for a pass that might lead us around the upcoming mountains. As we found on our last journey, the steeper the mountains get, the more challenging they can be to cross."

Boljie jumped right in, saying, "Yes, we made an extra long, unnecessary walk, climbing over the mountain. On the way back, we found a valley that took us right around the side of the mountain. We have a long walk ahead of us. No point in making extra steps!"

"I vote we camp here for a couple of days to replenish our supplies and to rest while a few parties set out in different directions each day to scout out the area. As soon as they are back, we can set course," Hamrock said to the group.

With this new piece of the plan in place, the next morning, three groups headed off in different directions in search of an easy route. Of course, Hamrock, Boljie, and Bikkram were right there to lead.

Before they headed off, everyone sat by the fire. It was essential to have guidance from their unfettered friends on the other side of the veil. Taking the time for attunement was a worthy delay on such a beautiful day.

The leaders had practiced over time, speaking with each other using telepathy as an aspect of this new level of personal expression. This would prove handy today!

Leaving behind the young ladies and a few of the men, the rest divided into groups. The leaders stood in their spot while the others chose which to follow. That done, they headed off to find the path to their new friends.

There would be a lot to chat about around the fire tonight!

Bikkram's group was the first to return. They had only been gone for a few hours.

"We got stumped," he said. We walked west for several hours. It was a simple walk as we stayed on flat land to see where it would take us. We watched for paths to go up, but saw nothing of interest.

"We caught a few rabbits along the way for dinner, but at the end, we found ourselves in a box canyon with very high walls. There were lots of plants that Klum told us we could eat, so we bagged them up. The walls were too much of a barrier for us to continue, so we came back."

"We think we found the trail!" said Hamrock as they rushed into the camp a while later. "There is even evidence of people using it."

His face showed concern as he continued. "I think it might have been the path those people who walked through our camp used. There is garbage all over the place. They did not even show respect to the animals they hunted. We will have to be careful and keep our energies high."

Evening set in as they relaxed and enjoyed the bounties of their day. The fires were so precious tonight, knowing their new friends were that much nearer.

Concern was mounting though as Boljie and his group had not returned. They had not even chatted with them through their minds. It was getting late enough that Hamrock reached out to them.

All he got back was an intense, warm feeling from the group.

"We have wasted no time getting into the rising land on this trail," Boljie said as they all laughed.

As soon as they began the climb, every member of the group could feel something shift in their energy. It felt good. A good they had never felt before.

The trees were of particular interest. The leaves shimmered and vibrated like something was shaking them. At first, it was just noticeable. However, the further they walked, the more clear it became.

"Have you noticed the animals, how they are acting as we pass by?" asked Pintu.

"Yeah. Rather than scurrying away, they stand there like they are saluting us. They just stand still as we pass by. They are not afraid. It is like they are paying tribute to us," said Boljie. "I wonder why."

After several hours of climbing a comfortable slope, the land descended into a beautiful valley. At their point of entry, they could see for miles, almost like eternity. It was breathtaking!

It was only a few hours since they had departed from the camp, so no one in the group felt it was necessary to check in with the others.

They just entered the valley and carried on as they continued their adventure.

"Look at the berries hanging from the bushes! They are huge, and they look delicious," Pintu said as she started gorging on the berries. The others were not far behind.

As they filled their tummies with the berries, they felt a sensation in their bodies. It felt so good!

The more they ate, the more the food energized them. Soon, they each sat down by a nearby tree (cedar, of course!) and fell asleep.

"I am Rachel. I serve the Universal God that created this earth and all that exists. I invite you to join me in this moment of knowing yourself through the eyes of God."

Not a movement stirred as they stared at this beautiful woman. They recognized her from earlier meditations, so they knew something good was about to happen.

"I am proud to welcome each of you to this valley. As you have felt the energy rise in your bodies, it shows that every one of you has done your work to elevate yourself as a spiritual being.

Relax now and let the energies work with you at soul level. If you choose, you may now ascend to a realm beyond your lives here on earth. You will leave the physical world behind and rise to a new vibration where you will have new abilities to help those souls still working at earth levels.

This is a very auspicious occasion. Meditate for some time and make your choice. Ask yourself if you are ready to leave the life you have known behind, and to forge ahead into an unknown experience that will offer you opportunities far greater than you have ever known.

Should you choose to not proceed, you may return to your families. Your life will be different, as you will still feel the changes. Your focus will be shared between this new level of energy and that of daily living. You may find it challenging at first, as the bliss you now feel will be ever present. It will pull on your ethereal body, asking you to ascend."

As they continued their meditations, one by one, their bodies shook as if they were having their own personal earthquake. They smiled and relaxed as they opened to their Ascension. Just like popcorn popping, they soon all disappeared. The valley became quiet again, in preparation for the next group, who were ready to move on to the bigger picture.

Chapter 20

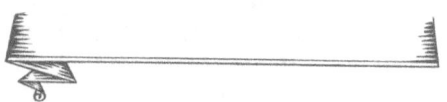

"We must be ever vigilant as we move forward today," said Hamrock as they assembled to prepare for the day's journey. "We are now well into territory that is unfamiliar to us, so it is important we keep our eyes open and energy up. Remember, positive energy wins the day."

With that, they all headed off with high expectations of being that much closer to their new friends.

During the night, Hamrock had a wonderful dream. He saw Rachel floating in the sky. She liked to appear just on the edge of a cloud as if she were a sticker on a page (except no one had invented stickers and pages yet!). He laughed as he thought about her being attached to the cloud. What if a wind came up and blew the cloud away, my beloved Rachel?

Rachel laughed with him. She liked silliness. It was good for the soul. It brought out the inner child.

Rachel showed Hamrock the scenery of the valley. He gasped at the amazing beauty that lay before him. It felt as if he was looking at eternity.

In the next instant, he saw Boljie and his group leaning against trees, meditating. Their faces were lit up with the most peaceful smiles one could ever imagine. He then saw each man vibrate and disappear. He knew they had transitioned to a higher realm and would not return from their walk.

It was a bit of a climb this day. Manageable, but still a climb. It was enough that they could feel the difference in their breathing, so the walk was quite slow. They were not in a hurry, so they just took their time enjoying the unfamiliar trees and plants.

They knew they were on a good road. The mess left behind was awful. They did their best to clean it up as they went, but there was so much! Today was beginning to look more like a garbage detail day than one of traveling on their journey.

Hamrock prayed as he walked. He asked the God of his Heart to clean this beautiful land and to help the people who disrespected the land to understand that protecting and valuing nature is vital to those who have been entrusted as keepers of our beloved planet.

He said to his fellow travelers, "I know it is frustrating to see this mess we find along the path. Please think of it as a test to help you be mindful of keeping your energies high. That is always the utmost desire. Positive thinking makes life work easier."

It was quite a long while before they crested the hill. At the top, they stopped to rest and embrace the scenery before them. It too was stunning, but not in how Hamrock had seen it in the previous night's dream. He was thankful, for, unlike Boljie's group, he did not wish to transition on this day.

They gave thanks for the wonderful bounty they had received along the trail as they prepared a scrumptious lunch of rabbit stew and a salad of fresh greens, and for dessert, baked pears! Yummy!

Every person was smiling so much that they had a hard time eating their food. The meal was so tasty. They truly felt blessed!

As they ate, a scene opened up to them not far away. It was not a picture that made their meal more enjoyable. Before them, they could see a group of people traveling. There were about fifty. Some of them were riding animals! This was exciting! Who would ever have thought?

There was no time for this bit of excitement, though. The people riding the horses were slave drivers. They were driving a large group of people trudging along the road. The slavers had tied these people together!

Hamrock and his people recalled ancient memories of being captured and driven into slavery. They would not let history repeat itself. What to do?

Leading everyone into meditation, they asked their God for an answer, pleading for the captured people to be freed, to live their true destiny. They sat in the quiet of the moment and waited... and waited, praying for the captors to become enlightened.

Some of the group became impatient. They wanted their God to act now. Hamrock cautioned them to stay quiet, even if it took days... or years.

"Just focus on your breath and be calm. Trust that everything will work out in its time," Hamrock said to the group.

The Wind Surfers watched as the scene unfolded. They, too, had been waiting for the scene to unfold before them. Now was that time.

Condor spoke to the horses. "Stay calm, my little ponies. Be still in your hearts. It is time for you to rest."

"What is going on?" said the gruff little man leading the parade, as the horses each laid down on the path to rest. He tried to spur his horse on, but the horse knew it was nappy time. No amount of prodding was going to change that.

The group came to a complete stop. Some of the captured people began laughing as their captors stood in frustration, looking at their sleeping horses. In fact, these people were so caught up with their horses that they forgot about their captives.

As soon as they realized they were no longer the focus, busy hands worked fast on the ropes. Freedom was theirs as they ran into the forest and out of sight. It was several minutes before the others realized their mission had fallen apart.

To make sure it stayed that way, Suzie appeared and led the people as far away from the scene as possible. She had already surveyed the area, finding a trail that led to a cave hidden behind a grove of trees.

Once inside, Suzie suggested to their minds they sit as quiet as a mouse. She led them in a meditation.

"Close your eyes as you make yourself comfortable. Focus on your breath and let it calm you as you slowly draw in your breath. Hold. Let your breath release. Hold. Keep following this pattern, then remain quiet."

Back at the horses, the people stared at the scene. How could things fall apart so? Everything was going so well... and then?

As Condor spoke to the horses again, the captors felt the last of their sanity melt. The horses rose together and sauntered off down the path, ignoring the calls of their masters. Freedom was their destiny, too.

Just to show how the excitement of their newfound freedom had energized them, the horses played some fun little horsy games as they strolled away. They snickered as they frolicked, making sure their former captors saw the fun they were enjoying.

One might say these folks were just a little upset. No horses, no slaves... and now they would have to walk to wherever. As their plans faded into the mists, they tried to find the trail where their captives had fled, but even the forest was against them that day.

They now realized they were all alone. Mission aborted.

Chapter 21

As the horses enjoyed their walk to freedom, Condor guided them straight to Hamrock and his group. It was quite a moment when they met each other. These people had never seen horses before, and the horses had never encountered people who didn't smell awful.

As they met, it became a party. The people hugged and patted the horses, speaking in quiet tones, reassuring the lovely beasts. As the horses enjoyed having their noses scratched, they relaxed and melded into the energy of the moment.

Condor smiled as he watched overhead. The Wind Surfers laughed and cheered sitting on the edge of their cloud. This was a fun role for our beloved gang.

On to the next step.

The Wind Surfers pondered the aftermath. The now horseless people needed to be removed from this scene. They were still a necessary part of the grand scheme, so they could not do them in with a bolt of lightning, or turned to stone or anything. (Besides, that would not be a positive choice). So, what to do with them?

As luck happened, these people made their own decision. Feeling so full of fear; they began running helter-skelter all over the place. They were all soon out of the picture as they tore up and over a hill. Several of them, being so fat and out of shape, had strokes and died right in the middle of the trail. The rest did not even bother to help their stricken comrades, they just continued running, even jumping right over these people, trying to outrun their fears.

As the situation cleared, Hamrock's people and their new friends moved from their safe nests. Even though the people who now lay dead on the ground had acted in an atrocious manner, they still deserved to be returned to the earth as their final moment in this incarnation.

One brave soul ventured from the cave. She wanted to find out if they could come out. With steps that barely graced the earth, she stole forward. Soon, she found herself staring at Hamrock's group, burying the fallen people.

Tisu felt safe right away as she watched the horses munching away on the grass in a nearby meadow. She stepped forward.

"I am Tisu," she said, using her quiet voice. She stood still until the others realized there was a newcomer in their presence.

"These people do not deserve to be buried with the dignity you provide. They have stolen the heart of our people. They were taking us to another land to sell us as slaves. We are thankful their time has ended," Tisu spoke in resentment.

A young lady, around Tisu's age, turned to her. Taking her in her arms, she consoled her with a big hug. Tisu broke into tears, as it sank into her mind, safety had returned.

The others had moved closer to the scene developing near the road. When they saw Tisu and the other young lady hug, they too came forward. In their hearts, they knew it was time for a celebration. They wanted hugs, too. It had been such a trial, a trial they never wanted to experience again.

"We must return to our village. These people left our old ones to fend for themselves. They said old people have no value. We know better, though. They are our storytellers and holders of our past. They wash away our troubles and offer wisdom for our future. Now, it is our turn to give back to them by returning to our home," Tisu said.

With that, Tisu and the others turned back for the return journey to their village.

For only a second, Hamrock, his group, and the horses remained still. Even the horses knew the next step as they prodded their new friends with their noses. Hamrock reached out with his open arms.

"Wait, this long journey has been to find you, so we are coming with you. We will not let you walk away now."

Tisu turned to look at Hamrock. "You have done us great service, although I do not know what you did to help us get free. We are not to be enslaved again, so please leave us alone."

Her statement confounded Hamrock. "Our desire is not to enslave you, my dear Tisu. We offer our hands in friendship. To travel with you back to your village, to help you and your elders to overcome this tragedy, and to give you strength to heal is our only desire."

"We know not this word, friendship. We have only ourselves. Until these men came along, we did not even know there were others. Now there are so many, it makes our heads swim."

"Until the recent past, it was the same for us. There are many more, we are told. The voice has guided us to discover other people, such as yourselves, to learn the value of friendship. We offer our hand in kindness, as your brothers and sisters," Hamrock offered.

Tata, the young lady who had consoled Tisu, spoke. "Did you enjoy the embrace we shared, Tisu?" She smiled as she held her hands out to her.

"I did," Tisu said as tears flowed from her eyes. "For the first time in a long time, I felt safe and valued as the person I am, not a thing to be sold." Tata bowed her head as her own tears fell. All the people in her group did the same. It was time for clearing the past.

Tisu took Tata in her arms. Hamrock and the others moved forward and created their world's first hugfest. The horses were not to be left out, either. Soon, all a passerby would see was one gigantic mass of people and horses embroiled together in one.

A new day had begun.

Chapter 22

Seeing the village as they came down a hill, Hamrock noticed it looked a lot like their own. The only visible difference was that no people were scurrying around.

As he looked at Tata. Her face told the story. No one asked questions.

Terrified of what they might find, all the villagers ran to their homes right away as if some kind of race had just begun. It was odd because, throughout the walk back to the village, these people almost needed to be prodded. Their walk was so slow, it was like they dreaded what they were going to find.

Once here though, holy smoke! There tore that last few feet like they were athletes.

Screams of delight shared with screams of sadness from others followed as each person peered into their home. It had only been a few days since the men had captured them and forced them away from their families. A few days can be a very long time for elderly people left alone, especially if they were not faring well, to begin with.

Tata and her people took to the jobs of looking after their people, consoling them, healing them... and burying them. It was a somber time at chez Tata.

Hamrock and his people jumped in to help. Some of their people were healers, so they set to work where needed. Others rebuilt fires, especially the main fire. They wanted everyone to feel like they were home again, to find that sense of belonging.

Since everyone would get hungry soon, Bikkram and several others headed off to find some dinner. A nice deer baking in an underground oven would cheer up the saddest of souls. Tisu was an expert on plants, so it did not take long for some nice wild veggies to appear at the main table.

Once the necessities were in place, everyone in Hamrock's group gathered around the main fire. It was time for a meditation and to give thanks. Tisu's people stared at them as if they were performing some kind of offbeat magic.

"What were you doing when you were sitting around the fire?" she asked Hamrock once they had returned to the outer world.

Hamrock looked at her, surprised. "At first we were giving thanks to our God, then we turned in further to meditate and reconnect with the Cosmic. Are you folks not familiar with such practices?"

"And so, tell me please, what do we have to feel thankful for? These people have stolen our lives and killed many of our elders. I feel so much hatred right now. I have no room to give thanks," Tata returned.

As he looked around at the villagers, Hamrock could see the hatred and disgust on the faces of each of them. He closed his eyes and prayed for them.

Taking the cue, Papi (you remember our beloved little butterfly?) transformed herself so she could come to their aid.

She flew low over the people, making sure they saw her. She flew some loops and a couple of dive bombs. Once she had their attention, she released her special gold dust that Rachel had blessed her with.

Everyone breathed in the dust as it flowed down. Soon, everyone was giggling like schoolgirls. There were even a few smiles. The energy in the village changed for the better as Papi flew in victory back to join the other Wind Surfers.

Later that day, once they had sorted all the elders out, everyone gathered at the fire. The villagers had warmed up somewhat to

Hamrock and his people, but they still kept their distance. This needed to change for the right future to occur.

Tisu invited Tata to sit with her by the fire. Tata liked her new friend, but her people had gathered away from the fire. As she sat down, she looked over at the others for reassurance.

Tisu put her arm around her friend and pulled her in close. They sat that way in silence for a long time. Sometimes words just get in the way.

It took quite a while, but the others began moving over to the fire. With everyone snuggled in, more than the fire was keeping them warm now. Hamrock stood and moved to the center of the fire area. It was time to introduce themselves and their mission.

"I am called Hamrock," he began. Then he introduced all the members of his party.

"We have made this journey to find you. Like you, until recent situations showed us otherwise, we thought we were alone. We have lived in our village for generations without knowing other people existed.

Through guidance from our Creator, other fine people have become part of our lives. These people who attempted to enslave you have passed through our lives as well. During our meditations, they instructed us to find others like ourselves, as it is now time to expand our community.

We wish to build a strong relationship with you that will last forever.

We can be stronger together, especially to protect ourselves against these predators... and we can learn to embrace these wonderful beasts that seem to enjoy our company."

He laughed as he looked over at the horses grazing nearby. As he looked at them, he visioned in his mind getting on one and going for a ride like he had seen the other people do. He smiled at the thought.

One beautiful palomino looked right at him, smiling a horsy smile. They connected at that moment.

Tisu then joined Hamrock in front of the fire. "We have learned that there are many communities like ours that are not yet aware others exist. It is our mission to find them and become friends. Our lives can only be better with more good people to share with. Would you not agree?" she smiled at Tata.

Soon, side conversations took over, so Tisu and Hamrock joined in what was becoming a verbal free-for-all. This was a time for connecting. Everyone stood and started chatting with whoever was nearest them. It was a little challenging at first, as the villagers were a bit shy. Soon it became easy to find things to chat about, since life in both villages was very similar.

Open communication replaced fears, and anxiety dissolved into the ethers while new friendships blossomed.

Hamrock and his people stayed with their new friends for a long while. It was easy to be here, now that the tension had dissolved.

The villagers found the rhythm of their lives again. Life became simple. They went on with their daily routines, filled with fun and laughter while sharing with their new friends. They hunted together and gathered plants together, sharing their knowledge of the many aspects of their lives.

Soon, it was easy to see. New special relationships had become apparent. Tisu's dream had come true.

It would have been so easy for everyone to continue living in this bliss, but Hamrock's people knew their mission was waiting ahead. It was going to be so much easier now that they were going to travel on horseback.

Having Hamrock and his group around for so long, everyone in the village was keen on building relationships with these amazing new friends.

Hamrock looked so gallant mounted on his palomino as members of both villages mozied along in search of the trail to the next episode in their adventure! It was hard to tell who had the bigger smile... Hamrock or the Palomino.

Chapter 23

They chose Tandoo to travel with Hamrock as spokesperson for his villagers. This new group was a mix of both groups, as several of the young ladies, including Tisu, had stayed behind for obvious reasons. The sisters of the brothers, who had found a new kind of bliss, replaced the bulk of her group. They hoped to find their own.

Similar to Hamrock's people, Tandoo only knew his land, never having felt drawn to travel beyond necessity. However, the excitement of finding new friends, and!!! Having horses to ride, were almost beyond tolerable levels for the poor chap.

They made a light camp when they arrived at the edge of their traditional hunting grounds. They needed guidance and some lunch.

Hamrock found himself a nice, quiet place to be alone, as some members prepared a lovely meal of rabbit and wild plants. That cedar tree looked so inviting, he thought.

(Goose smiled as he saw him lean back so, in fun, he leaned back against the other side of this wonderful tree.)

As he slipped into a peaceful meditation, Hamrock pondered the current situation. By first visualizing the group finding another village, he then saw them interacting with their new friends; sharing meals and swapping tales of hunting trips and life.

Sliding deep into the meditation, Hamrock never felt Tandoo sit down beside him.

When he opened his eyes, Tandoo smiled at him. It was obvious he had a question.

"What do you do when you are sitting quiet like that, my friend? You look like you are asleep, but I can see you are very busy."

"This is called meditating. I go inside myself so I can reach out to my God for calmness and to ask for help. I want us to find the route to the next village, so I go inside and make a picture of what my desire is, then I wait for the answer to come to me.

When we are ready to continue, something will tell us which path to follow. I trust with no doubt we will find our new friends."

"What is God? I have never heard of this person?" asked Tandoo.

"God is not a person. God is a consciousness. In fact, it is the collective consciousness of all consciousnesses. Everything that exists, including you and me, are aspects of God.

We are all connected, because we are all part of the one."

Tandoo pondered that statement for a few minutes, then asked.

"How does this God give you directions to the next village? Has he been there before?"

Hamrock replied, "Someone in the collective consciousness knows the answer to my question. There is a book called The Akashic Records that contains the everything of everything, so it is just a matter of tapping into it to find the answer. Either it comes to me in my mind, or a messenger may provide the answer."

"We have never learned to use such a tool. Can we learn how to do this too?"

"Yes, but tell me, my friend, is it part of your tradition to believe in a higher source?"

"The elders have spoken of spirits and other unseeable beings, but nobody listens to them. We believe that if one cannot see something, it is not real. However, ever since your people joined us, I have been watching you when you do this meditating, and I am feeling like it is something I am drawn to. I do not understand."

"If you are open to learning, I will teach you. Let's see if any of the others are feeling the same. I bet it is lunchtime now anyway," Hamrock said as he stood up. Patting his cedar tree for a moment, he turned with Tandoo and returned to camp.

"Before we continue our journey today, I have a question to offer each of you to ponder," Tandoo spoke to the group. "Hamrock has introduced me to a new concept. I am wondering if anyone else is feeling a draw to explore it. He calls it God. It lets him access information from beyond this world. It is how he is leading us."

"Why do we need to learn this if Hamrock is already getting the information? We can just follow him," one person asked.

Tandoo turned to Hamrock, who answered, "It is a good question. There are two answers, for now. First, it is important for you to establish your own relationship with God to get your own answers. You will learn to receive answers that apply to you alone, rather than using an interpreter who may give you biased information.

Second, you each have your own life path to live. To reach your own true potential, coming to terms to accept that having a relationship with a higher power gives you much more strength than limiting yourself to what your mind can provide to you on its own.

We are all connected through this higher consciousness. Through this relationship, we have learned to expand our knowledge of plants we eat or use for medicine, how to hunt better, how to live better and how to protect ourselves. And most important, to feel one with our land.

This might shock you, but these same men who were selling you into slavery came into our camp not long before we set off on this journey. They were looking for us. They wanted to do the same thing to us."

"What happened? Why did they not capture you?" asked Tandoo with a tone of excitement in his voice. His mind was churning at the new prospects.

"We have learned through our relationship with our God to raise our vibration through positive intention. By doing this, these men who vibrate at a very low frequency could not see us. They walked right through our village, even walking right through the main fire pit, without even knowing we were there. Can you imagine?" Hamrock laughed as he recounted the event his wife had told him.

The group was quiet for a few moments. They pondered what Hamrock had told them, but they felt nervous, too. This was information way beyond their understanding!

Continuing the thought, Hamrock added. "I know this is hard to believe, but it is true. It is only a few years ago that we felt just like you are feeling right now. We were fortunate enough to find some other people during a hunting trip that helped us to see the truth about ourselves. It has taken a lot of letting go of old beliefs, so we can do what we do today.

It was through this connection that freed you from those men. Through our connection with Source, we invited an intermediary to speak to the animals, asking the horses to lie down and go to sleep. You saw it happen, so you know it is true.

Part of our mission in finding our new friends is to help each of you to find your connection with Source. We have been told these men will be back. By raising your consciousness to a high enough level, we can leave them to enjoy their lower level ambitions by themselves.

We are going to teach you about the power of living in love, and to let the energy of fear take its rightful place. And that place is not running your life.

I am going to let you ponder my statements for a while and then we will break camp and continue our journey." With that, Hamrock returned to his cedar tree and the quiet.

As he leaned against the cedar tree, he asked himself, "What is it about cedar trees? I just feel so connected! Goose laughed to himself as he slipped inside.

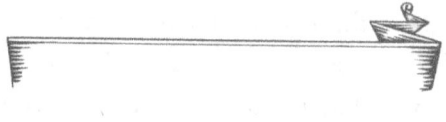

Chapter 24

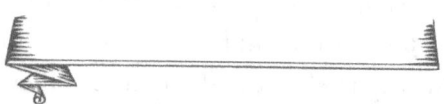

It was not long before Hamrock's point proved true. It had been an easy journey as they found their way over a small mountain. The trail appeared right before them.

And so did the people who had captured them before!

Somehow, they had re-equipped themselves with horses... and attitude.

Bikkram and Tandoo were riding ahead of the group to watch for any concerns when these people came into view. Riding back to the group, Hamrock had everyone dismount and find a nice comfy place to watch the upcoming event.

"Focus on your breath. Deep breaths in. Hold for a bit. Slow on the release. Hold for a bit. Then breathe in again. Keep repeating this process while seeing yourself radiating white light. Make yourself look like the sun," Hamrock led the group.

The horses knew what was going on, so they moved into the bush to find their quiet place. (Condor, Goose, and Raven joined them to help them have their own meditation.)

A few minutes later, these people strode right past them. The villagers all giggled to themselves as they watched them pass so close they could smell them. (Yuk!)

It sure seemed strange when their horses turned to look at the people sitting by the path, snickering as if they had been told a good joke. Once they were clear of them, they all laid down to have a sleep.

"Not again!" said one slaver. "What is it with this area that makes horses want to lie down to sleep? Is the air too thin or something?"

They stood there for a few minutes pondering the situation, trying to get the horses to resume their walk. No such luck!

"We are not running this time. I want to know what is going on here. We have a job to do, and something is interfering with it. I mean to put an end to this tomfoolery," one of them said as he attempted to pull his horse up by the bridle. Ya right!

Condor, Goose, and Raven were watching things unfold. They were not planning to intercede unless things got out of hand. It soon became obvious this would not be necessary.

Hamrock told everyone to remain quiet and to keep their energy up as they mounted their horses to continue their journey. As they rode away, the other horses got up to their feet, shook themselves off, and joined their new friends. They had new priorities that did not include these miserable and smelly people.

Now the slavers were in a fit, but they had no one to take their anger out on, so they fought with each other.

"Where are you going, you stupid horses?" was the last thing the horses heard as they laughed, trotting off, with a little heel kick in the air to express their newfound joy and freedom.

"Wow! That does work!" said Tandoo as they stopped a while later. "How come the horses could see us, though?"

"Horses do not have the clutter in their minds that humans of lower vibration have. They could sense our vibration. It appealed to them, so they followed their instincts.

Our horses may have been talking to them as well. Have you noticed that when we leave the horses alone, they all stay together? They look like they are having a chat. Maybe our horses called the other ones and told them to join us," Hamrock offered.

"Well, the more the merrier. Now we have enough for everyone to ride," Tandoo said as he jumped on his horse. Giving it a quick pat on its shoulder, and a warm word, they were off to continue this amazing journey.

(It was a good thing the Wind Surfers did not have to keep up with these folks, as they were rolling around on the cloud in fits of laughter. Raven almost fell off the cloud, he was laughing so hard!)

The path came to a split later that day, so they all decided that was enough riding for one day. They set camp up as several people headed into the forest to forage for their dinner. They camped in a pleasant meadow this day, so the edible plants were bountiful.

A nice yearling deer offered itself up only a short distance from the camp. The hunters had learned to show their appreciation for their success. After thanking the deer for giving up its life, they left the entrails in a clearing for other animals to feast.

Later that night, they could hear a real ruckus. It was so loud it woke everyone up. As they looked, they realized a pack of wolves had been munching on the gift left behind. They also noticed the other people from earlier in the day as they came into sight.

These folks had not seen the campers. They were just trying to find their way back up the road. However, the wolves did not like being disturbed during their meal, so they voiced their opinions to the offenders.

The people ran up the right fork of the trail with the wolves in hot pursuit. That was the end of those guys for a while. The last thing they heard was the leader yelling something about coming back to get even.

Done with their little job, the wolves returned to their dinner, they walked past the villagers. The lead wolf beamed with a proud look on his face as he looked at them. He laughed a wolf laugh at them, then ran to catch up with his friends. They would have a lot to chat about tonight after their bellies were full.

It was two full days of riding before Hamrock, and his group got any sense of other people. It was no wonder they had never gotten to know each other. And that was while riding horses! Can you imagine how long that would have taken walking?

At long last, they saw the smoke of a village in the distance. He recognized it right away. It was the home of none other than Portu!

They must have traveled in one large circle. Portu appeared in an instant to welcome them.

"Well, Hamrock, it is so nice to be with you again. I see you have learned a new lesson," she said, as she patted the flank of his horse. "We have never learned to ride these magnificent animals, as we can travel by other means quite well. They have served you well on your long journey.

There are so many of you now. Your mission is doing well. Come visit us for a while.

We have a special treat for you and everyone. Our friends from the future are visiting us."

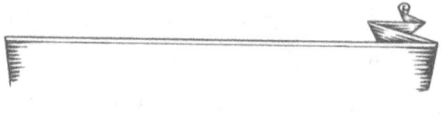

Chapter 25

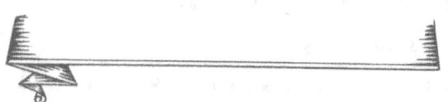

Portu's village had become one great big party. Everyone was there now. Portu's family, Hamrock's entire village, Tandoo's people, and now Suzie and the Wind Surfers. As a special treat, even Klum and Grey Eagle made an appearance.

This was turning out to be one special day!

To make it even better, as they partied on, Rachel made a guest appearance.

"I am Rachel. I serve the Universal God that created this earth and all that exists. I invite you to join me in this moment of knowing yourself through the eyes of God."

She smiled that special smile of hers at her friends as they each found a quiet place to rest in the sudden quiet. Even Tandoo's people knew this was an auspicious occasion.

"It pleases me so much to see each of you amongst your new friends. The energy you share is healing and soothing many of the fears that have driven your lives for so many generations.

It is through the love you share in the now that will empower the people of your future.

We will continue our work to peel off the layers of misinformation that have held you from meeting your greatest glory.

I invite each of you now to step past the veil. I invite you to experience what true freedom is, so that this may guide you, as you shape your life into the incredible journey it holds as a possibility."

As Rachel faded from their consciousness, Portu and her sisters handed out mugs of a special tea to each person. It was time for a special meditation.

Suzie stood to lead the meditation. She was almost beside herself with excitement. She knew the power of these mugs of Destiny Tea. This would indeed be a special treat.

She began, "This is an auspicious occasion. The tea you are drinking will help you relax. It will let you slip past the veil that separates this present life from eternity. You are safe, so just relax and enjoy."

With that, she sat down to join in on the fun. In only seconds, Papi was in her glory, flitting about with all her new butterfly friends. What fun! A butterfly circus!

Suzie remembered the dreams, so long ago when she, as Merle, first embraced the wonder of oneness with all. She smiled as she recalled that first time knowing and embracing her inner butterfly. Nothing could exceed this feeling. There was no greater freedom!

Merle opened her eyes as she sat with her people. They continued their butterfly journeys as she sat and looked at the faces of each person, seeing each one in the ultimate glory of this incredible moment. There could not be a more exalted moment in any person's life.

Feeling her return to consciousness, the Wind Surfers each opened their eyes. Leaving the others, as a group, they began to glow with an intensity so great one had to cover their eyes. Soon, the party in Portu's village shared nine fewer people. Instead, they soon sat in a meditation circle at the center with Reverend Harry and Rose.

"We were wondering why we had put out so many chairs today. Any time we set up, we put out just the right number, as the people we feel will show up. Good thing we trusted our instincts," laughed Harry.

"Yes, it would have been rather uncomfortable and embarrassing if we had landed in other people's laps!" said Goose, laughing at the thought.

Merle looked at Harry and Rose, smiling that same smile of Rachel. It had been quite a special journey for her as she recalled the joy of being Suzie.

She said, "How are things at Greenwood Commons? Did things get sorted out with the people camped at the front gate?"

Harry and Rose looked at her with a strange look. "We do not know what you are referring to, my friend." Rose said. "To what are you speaking?"

The Wind Surfers all realized they had accomplished their goal. They had completed their mission to rewrite the karmic history of the people at the gate.

"Some people whose ancestors had shared this land for thousands of years came to us some time ago," Rose said, trying to establish a connection to Merle's question.

"Some government officials had come to them, trying to incite them to create a situation with the people at Greenwood Commons. The government people said they wanted them to claim these newcomers were intruders on their territorial land.

We held a meeting right here in this room with these folks. They wanted to know the real reason these government people were acting this way.

The spokesperson for their group told us that, even though they had lived on these lands for many centuries, they knew all land belonged to the Universe. No claim or piece of paper could change that fact. The most we could ever do is make use of this land and look after it.

In fact, several of their families had purchased units in Greenwood Commons because they loved the energy there!

"We have been doing special meditations with them this past while. Their path to the other side of the veil uses different techniques from ours. By the way," Harry said, "Did you meet Klum and Grey Eagle on your journey?"

Everyone had a good laugh. Then they all got up and hugged in one enormous ball.

Harry then returned to his seat. He had a very serious look on his face.

Chapter 26

"I don't care how long it takes, even if it takes lifetimes, we are going to catch these people and make them pay," he said to the rest of his gang.

"Where could they have disappeared to anyway?" another man grumbled. "This has happened too many times now. We can't make our living selling slaves if they keep disappearing on us.

"They have to be here somewhere. Let's go back to the places where we lost them and see if we can find some clues."

With that, they mounted their horses. Retracing their trail back to the site where they lost their last set of horses, their minds wandered back to the scene of only a month ago.

By the time they found where they assumed the site was, they were all in a froth. These people, a much smaller group now, were feeling consumed with anger. (In truth, they were more embarrassed, but it was easier for them to feel angry!)

"With all these people bailing out on us now, how are we supposed to overwhelm the people in these villages? We need the numbers to take captives. Now there are just a few of us, and I don't even trust our horses to stay with us. We have our work cut out for us, if we are to keep going," the man grumbled again.

At the first site, they found nothing. After all, nothing had really happened there, except their horses had run off. Of course, then some wolves had chased the remaining people off since they were now on foot. They did not even both getting off their horses.

Continuing on, they never even noticed their horses snickering and kicking up their heels in glee. After all, one's focus on their life is often very limited when negative energy, like anger, drives them. Their anger ran their whole life.

It was not far to the site where they had lost the set of people they had captured to sell into slavery.

When they arrived at the site, they tied the horses up to make sure they did not wander off. Then they set off to explore the area, hoping something would make sense.

It took a while, but one of them found the cave. He yelled to the other guys to join him as he entered.

"This is how they got away, for sure. We got so caught up with the horses acting up, we never even tried to find them. That sure was a weird day!"

There was nothing in the cave to tell them where the people had gone, so they presumed they had returned to their village.

"They won't be so easy to fool this time, so we will have to be tougher on them this time if we are going to turn them into profitable trading assets.

They hurried back to their horses, setting off toward the village. Again, they did not notice the glee the horses enjoyed.

It took about a day to arrive where they thought the village was. They searched and searched the area. All they found was a large clearing.

"How could an entire village disappear? This is getting too crazy for me. Let's camp here for the night. Tomorrow we might as well go home," the man who liked to grumble said.

As they settled in, the energy of this location absorbed into their beings. By the time they were asleep, this new feeling had begun its work.

During their sleep, an angel visited them. She peered down at them from a fluffy cloud above. With the most beautiful smile, she said to each of them,

"I am Rachel. I serve the Universal God that created this earth and all that exists. I invite you to join me in this moment of knowing yourself through the eyes of God.

As you have seen, your choices have been contradictory to your happiness. With the new feeling that is growing inside you, you are given a choice.

You may continue to live in the energy of fear as you have for so many generations, or you may choose to embrace this new feeling of love.

This new feeling will empower you to evolve and join those whom you seek, who have now risen to a level beyond your current perception. You will then live in harmony with them and all others.

If you choose to continue as you have been, your load will remain heavy as you carry the weight of your past."

It was a long sleep that night. Since they were just heading home, no one was in a hurry to break camp in the morning. They let themselves sleep and sleep.

By mid-afternoon, faces began to show from under the blankets. No one spoke as they set about preparing a meal. It took a long time before any of those who frittered about in the camp realized they were fewer in numbers again... and the horses were gone!

"They left without us!" a few of the remaining people mumbled as they prepared to head off. "Now, what are we supposed to do?"

As they set off, no one noticed there were no fresh tracks of horses or men heading off toward their home. It was going to be a long, empty walk.

Several days later, this group stumbled into their hometown, unnoticed. Hunger pangs had joined them as they walked. Since these people did not know the wonderful bounty of food that existed in nature, they went without food pretty much the whole walk.

Even though they excelled as hunters, nature proved to be the boss again by keeping the animals at a safe distance so they could enjoy their choices.

As they stumbled through their town, trying to make it to their homes, people glared at the tramps who dared entered the sanctity of their paradise. The grumpy guy even tried to ask for help from passersby. All they received were glares.

The people in the town came to their rescue too late as they dumped the bodies of the last of the slavers in a hole at the edge of the city dump. They would not even give them the grace to be buried in the cemetery.

"I am going to bury these people for not covering for us," he said to his group of closest allies. The country's leader knew she was in a spot. She was determined someone else would take the fall.

"There has to be another way for us to come out smelling like roses. Let's get our thinking caps on and make it happen. The very existence of this country as a free state depends on the outcome of our ability to cover up this situation," she continued.

Each person sitting in the meeting knew full well the reality of what their leader spoke. They knew it because they had each been a perpetrator of the situation. They had not counted on it backfiring though, even though their bank accounts were the healthiest ever.

"We cannot print more money, as that will force a free fall in the world economy. Our country is producing as much as it can, so there is no room for expansion.

We need to enslave our citizens. We need to do it in such a way they will not realize they have become slaves, and we need to do it in such a way no one will blame us."

"How about if we create a cataclysmic event that knocks the country into a severe depression? We can make it look like a natural disaster caused it, then we can blame God," offered the leader's aide.

The leader looked at her and smiled. "You are a genius, my dear. That is why you have such a prestigious position in my cabinet. How can we do this?"

"I know of a machine that creates such a strong negative energy that it can cause Mother Nature herself to fall to her knees. We can direct it to a certain area and when they turn it up full, they will think Armageddon has occurred.

The whole natural cycle will fail, causing the area to fall into a wasteland. I know where to focus it on too!" she sneered.

Days later, the machine was ready to deliver. As part of their scheme, they had reached out to the plastic wood manufacturing business in the town where good folks at Greenwood Commons made their homes.

Dave was the president of the lumber mill. When he received the letter from the government telling him about the new power generator they were giving him, he was excited.

The mill had become so busy creating the wood from plastic and other garbage that it was faltering, as it was consuming more electricity than the current system could supply.

"We heard you were running into a challenge with the electrical supply, so since you folks contribute such a huge percentage to the economy, we felt we could contribute this machine to help you out. Please consider it a donation. We just want to help."

This was the reply he received when he contacted the government agency that was on the letterhead.

Dave called a meeting of the mill's board to tell them of the windfall.

"That is perfect. The mill is already running way past capacity. This will relieve the pressure. It can't get here too soon," was the reply he got from the head of the mechanical department.

"Not to be a pessimist or to poo-poo a gift from the government," Alice the comptroller said in a voice filled with hesitancy.

"As you all know from my many rants, I do not trust this government. I heard a rumor that they had tried to start an uprising with the indigenous people a while back. It failed, though, when these folks would not play the game with them. They said they were quite content with the way things were working right now and were not interested in starting problems with anyone.

My concern is this might be another tactic to cause a situation to replace that one. After all, it is so convenient that they offer us this gift when we are in the same area of the country."

Being that the policy of the company was to operate the board by consensus, they had heard Alice's statements. This lady was not a young pup fresh from college. Over her many years in the working world, she had endured the foibles of many governments. There was no such thing as a free gift from the government. Everything had a price with these people.

Speed in never in the equation, when the government is involved in a project. Discussions upon discussions with every department need to be held so everyone can get their two cents' worth into the situation. It was a surprise for Dave and his council when the low bed truck with the generator arrived in their yard less than a week later.

As the workers were unloading the machine into the power room, they met again.

Dave opened the meeting by saying, "Let's appreciate Alice's concerns. This is too suspicious. Is everyone in agreement?"

With instant consensus, they implemented a cautionary plan.

The head mechanical engineer took charge once they had placed the machine.

"We need to do a complete inspection of this machine before we power it up. A full analysis of its workings is a must, so we know what this machine is capable of."

It would take days for Tom to complete the investigation. It looked like any other power generator he had ever seen, so there did not appear to be an issue. However, he, like all the others, had his suspicions enough to not accept a free gift from the government at face value.

Now that the Wind Surfers and Merle were back from their journey to the past, life returned to normal for Rose and Reverend Harry. It just seemed so different with them not off doing their concerts or doing talks at the many other centers that had developed over the recent years.

Harry loved to muse about how his life had changed since those challenging days when the orb had tried to take control of his beloved region. He chuckled to himself as he reminisced about his past life, a place of comical attempts to control his limited life, according to someone else's beliefs.

Through his relationships with Rose and the Wind Surfers, he now found his life so fulfilling. He blushed to himself as pictures of the people in his fair town showed how a little change in belief can make such a dynamic shift in how life expresses for the better. He knew he had reason to feel good... in the most humble way, of course.

"Harry... Harry," called Goose. "Earth calling Harry."

Harry opened his eyes bit by bit. His mind wanted to continue its movie, but it was time to rejoin the planet, and a life moving forward to levels unknown.

Harry smiled at Goose, then he realized the whole entourage was sitting before him waiting, smiling as they enjoyed the look on his face.

"It looked like we had lost you to another realm for a minute there, Reverend Harry," Rose laughed as she took his hand.

"I was reminiscing about how all the people here, and how much things have changed around here."

"Well, the opportunity for things to get even better is upon us. It is time to put together a plan to make some changes in this government. Things are feeling a little wonky these days, wouldn't you agree?" asked Goose.

Harry smiled in agreement but remained silent.

"We can feel the negative energy in the air since we foiled their attempts to have the indigenous people take the fall to cover their attempts to hide whatever is going on.

Now that all is well in that business, let's start to find out the truth so we can fix this higher level issue. The first step is going to be investigating this new power plant. They want to kick it up at the mill today. The chief engineer found nothing suspicious, but just to be sure, Dave has asked us to come by to check it out, too."

With that, they all headed outside. It was a beautiful spring day, so bicycles were the mode of transport for this crew. They laughed and teased each other as Rose reminded them of the day a bicycle tour explored the town to find the site for the future Greenwood Commons.

On their arrival at the mill, the bicycles were abandoned on the ground. Sauntering up to the crowd, they joined into the milieu surrounding the power plant... anticipating the news.

This was Raven's time! Raven had taken a shine to doing remote viewing. Everyone knew this was a much more valuable and time saving procedure than having an engineer come in to disassemble the machine hoping to find an anomaly.

Raven closed his eyes, breathing in, focusing on the screen of his mind. In a couple of minutes, he had connected with the energy of the power plant. Standing right beside this piece of equipment to do this exercise turned out to be a poor choice as he soon found himself lying flat on the ground a few feet away, looking like he had touched a live high-voltage power cord.

"Wow!" he said as he opened his eyes. "That was harsh. And the machine is not even turned on!"

Rose was standing near him, so, as she helped him back up, she said, "Never mind not turned on, it is not even plugged in!" She showed him the main wire still lying on the ground, waiting to be attached to the breaker.

Rachel appeared above. She had been watching the situation with none of them knowing.

"Let me have a look from here. If this machine is what I think it is, we have already had this experience in the recent past."

With that, she began using her x-ray vision to scan the workings of this machine. The others closed their eyes as well, tuning into Rachel's channel so they could get a view as well.

It did not take long for the prize to appear. Hidden deep inside the machine, where no regular human could see it, was a box. At first, Rachel could not see inside it, as they had made it of a very dense material. Everyone knew they had hit the jackpot though, because it was obvious that this was an attempt to hide the true purpose of this gift.

Shifting gears, the insides of this box came into plain view.

"It is an alternator!" laughed Raven. "An alternator, but it is wired backwards, so it generates negative energy instead of the positive energy it requires to help run the plant.

As soon as we turned the machine on, it would start producing negative energy in huge amounts. We would be in for a small repeat of what we experienced with the orb."

Rachel smiled like a proud mom at Raven. "So what do you suggest we do now that we know the truth?"

Raven replied, "Let's all focus on this box, imagining its own collective consciousness, as minimal as it might be, repurposes itself into a turbo that helps the machine produce even more positive power than they designed it to do. Once done, we can scan the machine again to ensure this was the only gift."

The power of collective thought proved itself again. In only an instant, the little gift began its new positive purpose in life.

That job finished; they watched on the screens of their minds as Raven led them through a tour of the entire machine.

"Everything seems normal now, so I think it is safe to plug it in and get things happening," Raven said to the others as he finished the scan.

Dave walked over, picking up the power cord. He inserted the wire ends into their receptacles. Once he had tightened them into place, He said, "Hit it!"

The machine came to life, purring like a big old pussy cat. The machine now was a special gift as the mill shifted into production. It was easy to tell that this higher level of power was going to help the output.

"Now that we have fixed this event, how do we handle interacting with the government?" asked Rose as they reconvened at the Center.

"I say we send them a friendly letter thanking them for the power plant. We could include some pictures of how much more efficient the plant is working with the increase of power," offered Condor.

"Let's include some pictures of the workers smiling as they work too!" said Hummingbird as he began jumping around. "After all, they would want everyone to be happy with the gift, right?"

"That's a great idea. We will make no reference to finding their true purpose in the gift, then we will just wait and watch," Reverend Harry said.

Chapter 27

"We will just see how smiling their faces are when that box kicks in," she said as she glared at the photos. "If they think they can operate beyond our control now. Just wait, my little sweeties. You ain't seen nothin' yet!

Briach, I want you to head over there as an observer. Don't let anyone see you, and don't you do anything! Just watch them for a few days."

There was something about this town, something special, Briach mused as he sat in his camper van. He had found a nice hiding place where he could observe the whole mill. Although it was rather tedious sitting still for hours at a time, he found life at the mill very interesting. Trucks came with raw materials. Other trucks hauled away the finished boards. Workers at the mill operated machinery.

It fascinated him, watching the big trucks as the hydraulic platform lifted up the big, heavy trucks, leaving their noses pointed way up in the air as their load slid off into the hoppers. He thought that would be so much fun to be in the cab of one of those trucks.

It took him several days of just sitting to realize that life was normal. Nothing was breaking down. There were no catastrophic events. Even he felt the best!

This realization would not bode well for his report! Or, for that fact, his career!

Briach sat there lulled into a mindless state for several more days. Late one night, a visitor came. There was no knock on the window of his camper, but he reacted like she had, as she said,

"*I am Rachel. I serve the Universal God that created this earth and all that exists. I invite you to join me in this moment of knowing yourself through the eyes of God.*"

Briach just smiled as he embraced this wonderful vision.

"Simpa, I want you to head out and find out what is going on with Briach. He has been gone for over two weeks and has not reported back to me once," she said to her aide.

It took Simpa quite a while to find Briach's camper. He had hidden it very well in a forest just above the mill. Simpa had a quiet crush on Briach, so she hoped this would be a great opportunity for getting to know him better, and, together, to make names for themselves with her employer. What more could a girl want?

As she tiptoed up to the camper, she soon realized she was alone. Briach was not in the camper. She wondered where he might be as she opened the door and climbed in.

"He must have gone for a walk or something. It must be boring sitting here for days at a time. I will just wait here until he returns," she said to herself.

Simpa soon found herself mesmerized by the activity at the mill. The scene seemed so normal. Trucks arriving. Trucks leaving. She loved watching the big trucks rising in the air as their loads slid off into the hoppers.

"What's this?" she asked herself in a panic. "Is there someone riding in the cab of that truck as it lifts its nose in the air?"

And as fast as the thought entered her head, she realized it was Briach in the cab. She continued watching him for a while.

He would hide where no one could see him near the hopper. When the driver had placed his truck in the lift pad and stepped out, Briach would jump in the passenger side of the truck so he could ride up.

As the truck landed back on the ground, he jumped out to step back into his hiding place. It was obvious he was having the time of his life as he repeated this activity again and again.

Simpa did not know what to do at this point. He must have a reason for doing such a silly thing. How did this relate to his job as an observer?

She waited for his return. He must have a good explanation... she hoped.

It was hours before Briach made his return. Simpa was furious.

"Why were you riding up and down in all those trucks? I have been waiting here for you for hours! She will not be happy when I make my report."

Briach sat down in the camper as she prattled on. His mind was so peaceful, he could not even relate to her questioning.

"Well, Briach. What do you have to say for yourself?" Simpa continued, determined to cajole him into talking. Briach just sat looking at her with the most joyous look in his eyes.

"I talked to an angel," was all he replied. He then closed his eyes to meditate.

Simpa was not one to mess around with. This new behavior of her old friend and ally was not acceptable. Why would an angel come to talk with him, of all people, and who cares about what angels have to say about things, anyway? They had a job to do, an important one that would make an enormous difference in both of their careers... and now all he wants to do is meditate?

Simpa had been sitting in the front seat of the camper van. As she got up to knock some sense into her friend, she felt a thick energy push her back into her seat. Her attempts were fruitless. As long as she persisted in trying to stand, the energy held her tight. She even looked down to see if she had somehow put the seatbelt on. Nope.

Being a determined young lady, the struggle continued for several minutes. There came a time, though, when she gave up. She realized that whatever was holding her in place was much stronger than her.

Briach opened his eyes again. He smiled at Simpa. "I saw an angel," he said to her again.

"She is right above you, waiting to speak to you, too."

Simpa looked stunned at him. "What do you mean, she is waiting to talk with me? I do not see an angel, and why would she want to talk to me? I have no interest in what she has to say!"

Wow! If Briach's odd demeanor upset Simpa, this statement sent her into a rage. That was it! Enough of this tomfoolery. It was time to get out of here.

Simpa tried to stand up again. She could not. She was going nowhere, held down by a force unknown. It took a while, since tenacity was her middle name, so to speak, but when she realized there was no choice, she stopped struggling.

She felt exhausted. She closed her eyes. The tears began. She had never felt so powerless in her life. It reminded her of her childhood, when some bullies had pinned her down at school. They tormented her, calling her names, telling her she was worthless.

The tears flowed like a river. Simpa did not like being reminded that she was once powerless. For the rest of her life, her goal was proving to the world that she was a powerful person. There was nothing she would not do to prove she was strong. Even though she loved Briach, she would not let herself succumb to the weakening power of love. No, to Simpa, being strong was all there was to her life.

As the tears poured down her cheeks, she let go. She relaxed. She felt like she went unconscious. The energy that held her down released. She just sat there, exhausted from the struggle.

In her mind, the angel came to her.

"*I am Rachel. I serve the Universal God that created this earth and all that exists. I invite you to join me in this moment of knowing yourself through the eyes of God.*"

Rachel waited for a moment to let Simpa make her choice. Would she give recognition to an angel?

Simpa glared at her. "Why have you done this to me? I have no desire to know you. I must stay strong to protect myself. If I recognize you, I will become weak like you have made Briach."

Rachel smiled her most loving smile at Simpa. She waited for Simpa to relax again.

"*Life as a human is very challenging, my most cherished child. You have learned a tough lesson in this life that has reminded your subconscious mind of events that have occurred many lifetimes ago.*

It was an important event in this lifetime, for it is the fear that holds you to this event that must be released for you to become the powerful person you are born to be.

Standing in your truth through Universal love is the only true form of power. When your energy is big and strong because you flow in the energy of your Divine Source, then you will understand and express true power.

Your ego has created the dynamic illusion of power because it loves you. It is the only way your ego knows how to protect you. Your ego can never know God. Your ego is the devil within your being, for you are now living in hell.

It is your choice, my child. Do you wish to continue living in your self-created illusion of hell, or do you choose to let your ego release its hold on your life and become powerful as decreed by the God of your heart?"

Simpa continued to glare at Rachel. She had not heard a word she had spoken.

Rachel smiled again at Simpa and faded away.

Simpa sat in the seat for a long time. She could feel the power that had held her down was now gone, but she sat. She felt exhausted.

Her visit with Rachel only reminded her more of the struggle and the powerlessness she felt that day when the bullies had persecuted her.

Briach poured her a glass of water. He held it in front of her. She stayed quiet as he stood there. Would she take it? He hoped she had heard the message from Rachel. HIs heart yearned for her.

Simpa opened her eyes. Looking at Briach like he was a fiery dragon, she smashed the glass of water away with a stroke of her hand. She was free... and in a flash, she was gone.

Simpa ran like a person crazed by the sight of a demon. She had parked the car nearby, so it was a quick sprint. She felt so angry, so driven. Needing to escape this terrible, terrible ordeal was the only thought on her mind.

She felt so upset; Simpa struggled to get the key into the ignition. After a few tries, the car roared into life.

Foot to the bottom of the accelerator pedal, she was gone. Her zero to sixty was almost instant. She was on her way to safety... well, almost.

In only a matter of thirty seconds, she barreled right into the side of one of those big trucks lumbering along the mill road, with its big load of plastic garbage, heading into the mill. Some of the load lay atop her car.

Chapter 28

The angel came to her in a dream again. She said nothing. She just watched over Simpa.

"The girl is lucky to be alive. Had the truck been a little slower, she would have hit it right in the fuel tanks. She could have been burnt to death. As it is, she is in a coma, but she will be all right once she chooses to rejoin us. She took a pretty good hit to the head at the time of the impact. Other than that, she is okay," the nurse said to Reverend Harry.

Reverend Harry did not know this young lady or why she had been traveling so fast on the road by the mill. He did not know about Briach camping out watching the activities at the mill. He just knew this young lady needed help.

It had become his regular routine to check in on people at the local infirmary. It was so unusual for there to be anyone staying in the medical center. Ever since the orb fiasco, so many years ago, people did not get hurt very often. The town hospital had closed because of lack of necessity, so they opened an infirmary in its place. (It also doubled as a daycare center, just so the staff had something to do.)

Harry recognized in his own life how costly mistakes that caused so many accidents ceased to exist now that he lived such a calm and conscious life. He just did not make space for accidents. So many others had altered their lives to this concept as well.

However, today, this girl needed help. The medical staff jumped into action as soon as they heard about the accident. Although they felt bad for the girl, they were glad to get to play doctor for a while.

The nurse in charge searched the girl's belongings for some identification. They felt because she was unconscious, this would be permissible. She did not have a purse or a wallet on her person.

The administrator sent an ambulance attendant back to inspect the car she had been driving to see what she could find. The only evidence found was the registration for the car.

When the head nurse read the registration, she contacted Dave at the mill.

"Hi Dave, I thought you might appreciate knowing that the victim in the accident that occurred today at the mill was driving a car owned by the government. We could not identify her at all, but it felt important to reach out to you."

"Thanks, Mary Beth. That indeed is of concern. I will send a crew out to scour the area to see if we can find out what she was doing there." Dave hung up his phone. In the next breath, he dispatched a team to investigate.

It only took a few minutes for the team to follow the car tracks back to where Simpa had parked the car. The camper was in plain view.

Entering the camper, they found Briach. He was still sitting in his seat. He was still meditating.

The camper shook a bit as the men entered, so Briach opened his eyes. With the most peaceful look on his face, he looked at the men, then said, "I saw an angel."

With that, he closed his eyes again.

The investigators took pictures of the camper and its location, so they had evidence for later. They took note that the camper was facing the load dump and the mill.

Once they felt their work was complete, one man drove the camper down to the mill. As he parked it in the parking lot, he realized this was going to be inconvenient for everyone because the parking lot was so small. You see, most of the workers at the mill rode their bicycles to work because they liked to get exercise and breathe fresh air. The camper would be in the way of the bicycle racks.

He found a place out of the way near the truck dump. As he parked it, one of the truck drivers came to him. "I saw that camper up top there, but paid no mind to it. Thought it was just someone having a bit of time in nature. Then a few days later, I noticed a guy hanging around the dump, thinking we did not notice him.

I reported this to Fred up in the dump management center. Fred watched him jumping into the trucks as they were being lifted up to unload. The man seemed to get a real kick out of riding up and down. Although it is against the safety rules, Fred let him play. This went on for hours until the mill shut down for the day. He never saw him again."

When they checked the camper, the investigators found both Simpa's purse and Briach's wallet lying on the table. Now they had a reason for concern.

Once Dave received the report, he turned it over to Rose. "It seems that our beloved leader sent some spies to see how their gift was operating. One person is in the infirmary, the other is not lucid. He just keeps saying over and over that he talked with an angel."

Rose knew this was important news, so she closed her eyes and called the Wind Surfers. In a flash, they were sitting in the chairs at the table. Filling them in on the details, they agreed the time had come for some action.

"The first item on the agenda is to help this man return to consciousness. It must have been Rachel that visited him," said Goose.

"She sure does have an effect on people, doesn't she? She might have had a part in the actions of the girl in the infirmary as well!" laughed Condor. As he said this, everyone could hear a giggle from above.

Rachel popped in for a moment just long enough to say, *"Free choice is a tough thing to live with. Yes, I spoke with these precious individuals.*

They reacted in their own ways. Now they have the choice which path they will take to heal their lives."

As the meeting continued, Reverend Harry joined them. Upon hearing about the young man, he headed over to the infirmary to help him.

Mary Beth met him at the door. "They brought him in just after you left. He has no injuries, so we left him sitting in an armchair in the staff lounge. He appears to be meditating. The only thing he has said is that he talked with an angel, then he smiles and closes his eyes again."

Reverend Harry understood right away what had happened. The man needed to be grounded. His conscious mind could not cope with the experience of Rachel's visit, so it checked out, leaving him unable to function as a normal person.

Two staff members entered the room and lifted Briach onto a gurney, so Reverend Harry would do a treatment on him to help him get grounded. He hoped that once this was complete, he could answer some of the many questions about the new situation.

Harry stood at the man's feet as he lay there. He placed his hands on Briach's feet. He then started managed breathing to bring up his energy, and to connect with his patient on an energetic level. The next step was to pull down the man's consciousness back into his body.

Although Harry was a first-rate healing practitioner, it took a while. The man enjoyed being off in space and had little desire to come back. Harry connected with his mind in a sacred space.

"My friend, we know it feels so wonderful to be in the space you now enjoy. It is such a special event in our lives when Guardian Angel Rachel visits us. However, your life is waiting for you. I ask you to please make the choice to re-enter the mundane world."

"But why?" the man asked. "I am enjoying this bliss so much. I just want to stay here forever. There is nothing for me now in your world."

On that note, the man took a deep breath and joined this beautiful angel.

Even though Reverend Harry had experienced a person's transition across the veil several times before, he had never been connected to the person in this way.

"What a ride!" he told Rose later over coffee. "There we were chatting and with a single breath, he left his body. It felt like I was attached to a large elastic band. I could feel the band stretch and stretch until he shot right out the top of his head. One last breath and I saw him sitting before Rachel. I bounced back into my own body just as fast.

I could have gone with him. In fact, I could feel the pull. However, Rachel was watching, as ever. When she saw me coming at her, she put up her hand and sent my soul back into my body. It was a good thing my silver cord stayed in place so I could return.

What a rush, though!" Harry laughed as he reminisced about the event.

Rose laughed with him, then said, "It is good that he made his own choice. However, we have now lost the opportunity to find out what he was up to. We can only hope this girl will come back to consciousness soon so we can chat with her.

No such luck. The girl lay comatose for a couple more days, then one morning as the morning shift came on duty, they discovered her gone.

It seems one of the staff had placed her belongings in the drawer of the night table beside her bed. When she woke up, she found her phone and called her people. They could not get to retrieve her until the following day. She pretended to be unconscious so no one would attempt to interview her until her people broke in and helped her make her escape in the middle of the night.

Now they had no opportunity to find out what they were up to. Or did they?

Rose and the Wind Surfers met again. They had news to share.

"While she lay in bed, I checked in on her to see if I could find out anything," Rose said as the meeting began. "She was resistant to reveal anything to me at first. She just yelled at me, telling me meeting one angel was too many already and that I needed to leave her alone.

I withdrew to think about another tactic that would not upset her so. As she slept, I tried again. You would be so proud of me, Papi. I came to her as a butterfly. I saw myself sit on her shoulder as she lay there flapping my wings until I got her attention.

She opened her eyes. At first, she was gruff with me. As I flapped my wings, she relaxed. At the right moment, I connected with her mind, and she spilled the beans.

It seems that the man who has now left this world had been sent to spy on the mill. The leader wanted to know why nothing had changed since we turned the gift machine on. He had sat there watching for days, but found nothing unusual to report. The leader became concerned by his lack of reporting, so she sent this young lady to find out what was going on.

Rachel then filled in that she had visited each of them. "*The man had chosen to go his way while the girl, rejecting my offer, headed off in a manic rage in her car, thus causing the accident.*"

"We can expect a further visit soon then if they have the girl with them," Raven said. "We better be aware and prepared."

Condor then said, "Let's check in on them at their office. If we can get a heads up on their plan before they take action, we might be able to diffuse it."

With that, all eight of the Wind Surfers disappeared from the meeting. Harry laughed his usual nervous laugh. "I just can't get used to the idea that humans can make themselves disappear in one place and reappear somewhere else, like magic."

Rose laughed at Harry, then said. "It was like when we created the center, my friend. Do you recall how you felt so nervous about how quickly the center was transformed?"

"Yes, you told me the only difference was time, and that Jesus was a really good carpenter."

"Well, projecting from one place to another is the same. It is just about managing time and space. If they had gotten up and walked out of the room, they would have still disappeared from your consciousness, right? They just walked a bit further, that's all."

Harry just smiled his nervous smile as the concept sank in. There were still things Harry's mind could not yet grasp.

Chapter 29

Simpa sat in the interview room at her office. Simpa knew She was not happy.

"This was supposed to be a clandestine operation. You two bungled this up so much. Now they know we are up to something. And we still do not know why the power plant is not giving off the negative energy. Did you learn anything? And where is Briach now? He has just disappeared."

Simpa told her what she knew. It was not much. She did not know that Briach had chosen to leave this world.

"I only tried to talk with Briach in the camper. All he told me was that he talked with an angel, over and over again. I got mad at him because he was acting so stupid. When I tried to bring him back to reality, I could not get out of my chair. Then an angel talked to me, but I told her to go away.

After the accident, I fell into a coma for a long time. Some strange dreams kept playing in my mind. It was like we all had all been together in another lifetime, a long, long time ago.

We work together today, just like we were back then. I saw you as our leader then too, Madame President, but in the dream, we were men.

We made our living by raiding villages, taking people captive, and then selling them into slavery. We lived very well as we plied this trade. There was a lot of demand for slaves, but not many people to employ in this trade. Villages were very sparse and far apart.

The dream recurred many times in my slumber, revealing more each time. In the end, we ran into trouble when we captured people in this one little village. As we were forcing them to walk to their new home, something happened.

We had been riding horses so we would not get tired. As we rode along, the horses decided to lie down. They refused to get up. As we tried to deal with this problem, the slaves made their escape. Once the people were gone, the horses got up again and ran away.

From then on, we had nothing but trouble. We went back to their village but could not find it. All we found was a clear grassy spot. The next trip out, our new horses kept acting up like something was spooking them. Then, as we were walking along the trail, these horses run away too. The next thing I saw, a pack of wolves put the run on us.

Just before I woke up, I heard you yell, I will get you for this. We are not finished yet. No matter how long it takes."

She looked at Simpa. She pressed a button on the intercom. "Security, please come to my meeting room." Two minutes later, Simpa found herself enjoying the sights availed to her on the front porch of the building, her back to her former employer.

The Wind Surfers had crowded into the meeting room just before the leader had arrived. As the events unfolded, they chuckled as they wondered how She would react if She knew they were sitting there, listening in on the conversation.

"That girl sure took a hard hit on her head in that accident," She said to her newly promoted aide. "We don't need that kind of talk around here. I mean, seeing us together in another lifetime. How ridiculous.

Let's get back to work. We have a lot of slaves to sell today!" She laughed at the thought.

This event at the mill caused an immense problem for Her. After all, how was one supposed to carry on a clandestine operation after this fiasco?

She pondered this problem for quite a long time.

"An embargo! If we cannot be sneaky, we will be obvious! What a genius I am!" She thought to herself. "Now, just to figure out a reason."

Calling in her chief scientist, she laid out her idea. "That mill has become the primary source of income for that region. I need a reason to shut the mill down. Figure it out and get back to me asap."

He was a pretty smart guy, and he enjoyed being the Chief Scientist. She was his kind of woman, so he was determined to figure out this minor problem. Anything to be close to her. He fantasized as he pondered the situation.

It did not take him long. He flew back to Her office once he had it.

"The plastic they use as the basis of the wood develops a mold in it once it is mixed with solid material and heated. This mold can be detrimental to people's health. The mill needs to be shut down so we can investigate!" he said, sliding into his seat.

"Fantastic! Let's get the ball rolling!" At that, She pressed the intercom button calling in her aide.

By the end of the day, they were ready. The next morning, an entourage of police and investigators would be waiting at the front door of the mill.

"They are going to be in for the surprise of their lives! I am going to get these people under my control yet. Who do they think they are, anyway?" She mused out loud before the scientist and aide.

Back at the mill, the Wind Surfers breezed into the office. Dave knew there was some important news if they showed up unannounced.

"Hi, guys! You must have something important, so let's talk." He looked out the window at the parking lot. "How did you get here today? Did you walk? I don't see a car or any bicycles?"

They all just smiled but said nothing. To avoid the situation, Condor started the conversation. He reiterated what She had said and was about to do.

"I just do not understand why it is so important for her to have so much control. We need to ensure She does not get re-elected next round," Dave said.

"Well, we are going to have to play this out for now. Any suggestions what to do for when these folks show up tomorrow?" asked Goose.

Hummingbird, always one filled with off-the-wall ideas, jumped into the conversation.

"Let's have a pancake breakfast out front tomorrow with a big welcome sign for them!"

Everyone reacted on the spot. They thought at first that Hummingbird had lost his mind. But then, they realized the genius of the idea.

The next morning, everyone employed at the mill was outside. The parking lot looked like a fair was in town. In fact, the motorcade had to park on the road since the parking lot was so busy.

The Chief Scientist was not pleased. His fantasy of roaring up to the front of the mill with lights and sirens blaring was foiled. This was not how he had envisioned the start of this day.

He groaned and stepped back as he exited his limousine when he read the sign hanging at the entrance to the drive.

"Welcome Chief Scientist. We love you."

"That was a special touch, adding the funny little characters doing science experiments to the sign, Hummingbird. He should like that!" said Songbird to his buddy.

The police officer in charge of the event led the brigade into the parking lot.

"We are here to enforce a shutdown order for this mill," he shouted. He had intended to place the document right into Dave's hand, but there were so many people in attendance, he could not even get near him.

The officers were told to form a line around the crowd to be intimidating. The chief smiled to himself, as he said to the scientist, "This always works. We will just keep stepping forward until everyone is feeling squished. I will then demand the mill manager to surrender his authority to me."

Sounded good in theory, but the officers had not had breakfast yet. They had planned to head back to a neat little restaurant back on the highway home to celebrate their victory.

As the officers made the circle around the people, the smell of bacon cooking rose into the air. Then, is that pancakes? Oh, and hot maple syrup? Saliva poured into their mouths.

The people closest to the cooking area turned away from the police officers. The officers did not like having backs turned to them. They started pushing their way in to make the crowd tighter, but that food smelled so good!

The people grabbed plates. They filled them up with the great smelling food. Were they going to have breakfast? What about the police action that was surrounding them?

The police officers were feeling a lot of confusion. They wanted these people to recognize their authority, but, oh, that food smelled so good!

The people with the plates of delicious food spread out, filing to the outer perimeter of the crowd. One by one, they offered the plates of food to the officers.

Smiling as they handed them plates, all they said to them was, "Would you like coffee?"

As the officers broke rank, the police officer in charge and the scientist groaned and stepped back. Their authority, diffused by the smell of breakfast!

Now all they wondered was when theirs would arrive. After all, they were hungry too, from all the energy burned up from feeling important.

Returning to their car, they knew defeat was theirs. They needed to come up with a new strategy.

"This bacon is so good!" laughed the chief scientist. "I hope they are going to feed us like this every day we are here!"

"How did they know pancakes like these are my favorite way to start the day? Even the strawberry and the whipped cream topping is how I like them!" claimed the chief of police.

So much for developing a strategy! After all, who can connive with their mouths full of delicious food and special coffee?

They were so caught up in eating their breakfasts; they did not even note the fact that the other officers were now milling in the crowd, laughing as they enjoyed the most wonderful breakfast ever.

Little did anyone know; they had another visitor. Simpa lurked just far enough away that no one took notice of her. She wanted her job back. She would do anything to achieve this goal. Pancakes and bacon would not interrupt her plans!

But what is this? What is that incredible music?

We know what has happened, don't we?

A crowd and the Wind Surfers can only mean one thing. Party Time!

Nobody thought it was odd that these people just happen to have their musical instruments with them. Before long, nobody even cared. There was music and there was dancing!

The police chief and the scientist remained in their car, well, for as long as they could, anyway. Soon, everyone, and I mean everyone, was dancing. And who was right in the middle of the dancing? Simpa! And she was right in the arms of the chief scientist.

With everyone swooshing around the parking lot amid a Strauss Waltz, today's plans for anything else were done. There was always tomorrow.

Chapter 30

You think She felt angry before! Her poutiness was magnified a million times when, not only the chief scientist, but all the police officers quit their jobs. After all, what was the point of bothering these fine people just because She wanted to control them? They were doing fine on their own without her intervention.

"Hello, General. This is your boss." She said into the phone.

"We have an insurrection. Call out your men," was all he heard.

Instructions in place, the General led the convoy of soldiers. Standing in the open jeep, holding onto the staff of his huge regimental flag flapping in the wind, he smiled with delight. HIs time had come! He was getting the action he had dreamed of for so long.

All his career, he had sat at his desk. He even had a long table at the side of his office. It contained plastic soldiers and cannons and other instruments of war. He often spent hours strategizing how he would lead his men into battle.

Today was the day. His glory was shining brighter than the sun in the sky. The situation was unfolding as he had envisioned; leading his men into war. He was one happy puppy!

The soldiers were excited, too. They had heard about the great party that caused this momentous decision. In their minds, they hoped it was still party time.

When they arrived near the mill, the General ordered his convoy to halt.

"Men, this is an insurrection. These people have defied the government. It is our duty to quell this insolence." The General was also quite a gifted speaker. After all, he had been an active member in Toastmasters for many years, practicing for this day. He was in the Now.

The men formed behind the General in wide lines. It looked like this was more like a re-enactment of the Scottish Uprising in 1745 than a modern military action. But who was to know? After all, no one present had ever been in a war before.

Have you ever heard the question:

What would happen if the government declared war, but nobody showed up?

Well. Today was that day!

As the General yelled for the men to attack, the soldiers dropped their weapons to the ground. They did charge though... right into the dancing!

As they joined the party, a line dance song was just beginning. It was tough for everyone to do the steps, but they managed. With an extra hundred dancers in an already full parking lot, moving at all was a struggle. Nobody cared though, they were having fun.

By the time the General arrived at the point of engagement, he was alone. Every soldier had abandoned him. He was so disappointed! His time in the sun was now snuffed.

The General knew there would be trouble back in the capital. This was not the outcome She desired. What was he to do?

Sliding into the arms of a beautiful woman as a Waltz began, his woes melted. Recalling his early training in officer school, it was soon obvious; he was the best dancer on the floor!

The dancing went on forever; it seemed. The pancake breakfast became a smorgasbord lunch, then spaghetti cooked in a huge cauldron for dinner with delicious dinner buns and salad. Even a mini-donut truck arrived out of the blue!

By sundown, the whole town was dancing.

The dancing may have brought great joy to the folks at the mill; however, one person was not at all joyous. There was not a word that could describe how she felt.

She went home to her empty house that night, exhausted from the emotional turmoil she had experienced. As she sat down before her television, she popped in the video delivered by an unknown courier to her office earlier that day. She hoped it would be good. As the story revealed itself, She collapsed into a coma from sheer shock of the presentation.

Rachel loomed overhead. She knew no person could endure the insults to their ego this woman had endured this past day. Rachel also knew this was a perfect time for her to visit.

Rachel watched for a long time overhead, doing nothing, not interacting at all with the leader. This person carried a great deal of karma from her past. She also carried quite a load from her current position as leader of their country.

Rachel knew the unconscious memories prattling about inside her head maintained order through their strength. If this order became disturbed, she could suffer a mental breakdown of unparalleled proportions. This would serve no one.

This was going to be a subversive project. Rachel preferred to be upfront and visible, but that would not work in this case.

Rachel released a warm tide of golden energy. Start with a gentle stroke, she thought to herself. Release the burden one layer at a time. Even universal white light would be too much for now.

She smiled in love as the tide flowed over this woman. Tonight, all she would offer was peace.

However, this woman's ego had other plans!

Her ego recognized this new threat and was having no part of this business. It was in control. There was no discussion needed!

Rachel continued wafting the tide of golden energy over her. She visualized it forming a nice comfy blanket over this person. She saw her snuggle in, safe, like a caterpillar in a cocoon.

Nope, ego was not going for this! No comfy blanky for this one!

Rachel watched the wrestling match for hours. A time came much later when she let go. The fight had exhausted her. Calmness overtook her. She slept... for three days!

Simpa stayed hidden in the trees above the mill. Today was a far more entertaining day than the last time when her friend Briach sat staring at the trucks unloading at the dump.

Today, her first entertainment was the arrival of the police and the scientist. When the police officers abandoned their duties in favor of breakfast, she returned to her car to get her movie camera. Hope filled her while the film rolled on, as she dreamed of receiving the praise she so desired from the leader. She would get her job back.

Tripod set up. Camera mounted. She filmed the activities for hours. Imagine! Dancing! Simpa beamed.

She was in virtual ecstasy when the army arrived! Now these people, these infidels, were going to get their comeuppance! See, there is justice in this world!

Simpa almost knocked the video camera off its stand as she fell in shock. She watched the army arrive and fall into formation. The General looked so eloquent and polished, giving the men his speech. Who could not be motivated to quell this disobedience after such a great oration?

As the soldiers ran toward the event, the rifles dropped to the ground. Simpa passed out in shock. She just could not believe her eyes! Was there no end to this tomfoolery?

There was business to be done here, but all she saw was play. The final straw for her was watching the General move into position... to dance. Simpa had enough fodder now to become the highest ranking employee in the government. Yessiree, she was going to be back where she belonged, right at the side of the Anointed One.

Simpa was not a person who was very conscious of herself or her body. (Who could be with the desires for life expression she carried?) Simpa did not notice her feet tapping on the ground, moving to the rhythm of the music. A little pirouette through the trees would be okay, wouldn't it?

Soon, a battle raged inside her. She knew her career depended upon finishing gathering this evidence and getting it to her leader, but this music!

It was late afternoon before she tore herself away from the scene. It took a great deal of determination to do so, but she did get the movie stored in the trunk of her car. Taking her time while driving away from the mill, Simpa was feeling a little skittish about interacting with any more large trucks. She did not want to endure another visit with that angel!

Returning to her home, she found sleep challenging. She was so excited about her future. The video, dropped off at her former employer's office, created a level of excitement that overrode her desire for sleep. As much as she tried, sleep was not on the menu.

The next day, she waited on pins and needles for the phone call that would resurrect her career. It did not come.

The second day came and went. Simpa's need for sleep became victorious over her ego's enthusiasm for the future. She slept most of the second day undisturbed.

By the third morning, she was fit to be tied. Why had she heard nothing?

She had checked the camera as needed while the filming proceeded. She knew it had recorded the entire event. Why had she heard nothing?

Having been the personal aide to the leader, Simpa had been to Her house several times. She decided to go right to the source. This situation was growing old. She was losing any momentum sitting here, biding her time. Now was a time for unparalleled action.

Arriving at the leader's home, she almost pushed the door buzzer through the doorframe. A servant flew to the door to stop this objectionable racket. After all, She was sleeping and had left instructions She was not to be disturbed.

Simpa was having none of this. It was time to take the ball in this game and run for a goal.

Simpa barged into the TV room. She saw the leader sprawled on the couch, face down, right arm hanging limp toward the floor. She appeared unconscious.

Was it compassion? More likely a drive to get the ball rolling in this girl's case, but Simpa squatted on the floor beside this lifeless manikin. She stroked the woman's head in the most gentle manner, hoping to arouse her. She did not respond.

A servant had been standing in the doorway observing Simpa. When the leader did not respond to the girl's touch, she phoned for an ambulance.

Simpa stared as she watched her Eminence taken away. Now, what would happen to her career? Everything rode on receiving recognition from this woman. Or did it?

Chapter 31

It had been over a week since She had arrived in the hospital. Still unconscious, the world went on without Her.

Simpa had sat by Her side for a whole day, praying She would wake up. By the second day, she realized this could be a pivotal moment in her career. The country needed a leader.

It had not been that long since her dismissal. She hoped the administration had not processed the paperwork yet. It was time to find out.

Sneaking past the security, Simpa rushed into the elevator. Whew! First challenge out of the way. Make note of inefficient slackers at the security desk. She was already taking charge in her mind.

Where the heck was everybody? This place should be crowded with slaves pillaging stacks of papers. Maybe this is better anyway. No one present meant no one to see her.

"Oh, there they are, coffee time," she thought to herself. "But everybody at once?" She would never tolerate that as she cringed from the laughter rolling from the cafeteria!

The target revealed itself as she rushed around the corner. No one had seen her. They were all too busy jabbering with each other.

"Must be in her desk, if it is anywhere," she thought as she entered the room. And there it was! Her dismissal papers. And what's this? Her paycheck? She could use some cash right now.

Slipping the cheque into her pocket, the rest of the papers slipped like water over a waterfall into the shredder.

That done, she was now back on the payroll. First step in the new plan, completed. What would be the password to the computer? This was the next big obstacle.

Simpa knew that She was not very technical, so the password would either be quite simple, or it was written down somewhere. Searching the desk, she found a Rolodex inside a box on the desk. It contained a file card on everyone imaginable, and on the bottom of the box...

A funny-looking word on a post-it note.

It only took a moment to find Simpa's file on the computer. She laughed as she moved with grace and ease into her file. She knew she was much smarter than her now former employer.

With a minor change to her job description saved to the main server, and a huge pay raise, of course, she moved on to the next task.

The leader's file folder was very large. It contained every shred of information about her job and the overall operation of the country, so it took a bit to find the file Simpa was looking for. But there it was!

A little name change, inserted into the Transition of Power file in the Power of Attorney folder, and Simpa was golden.

The staff at the hospital kept the president sedated, making no effort to bring her back to consciousness. They felt it was best to let her return on her own.

Simpa visited her, sitting at her side for hours each day. The staff was pleasant to her, as they thought she was being a caring friend. They did not know what was going on in Simpa's mind.

Deep inside the catacombs of the leader's mind, she recalled. Her ego relaxed as it felt she was safe and under its control, so it let the pictures flow. It thought they were just meaningless expressions of the drugs the staff gave her.

She recalled all the victories of her leadership. Her ego jumped for joy at each picture. It gave little credence to the feelings that ensued.

The pool of emotion that sat on the floor of her mind grew with each change. Her mind reached further back. What foolishness were these pictures? She had never ridden a horse. And why were there people being pulled along beside her, trudging like slaves heading to market?

Her ego was enjoying the movie, as it realized the power She carried herself, like a queen in this scene, riding high on her beautiful palomino above these drivel of human dregs.

She looked around the landscape as the story unfolded. She recognized that person on the black horse behind her.

"What was she doing in my dream?" was all she had time to think as the horses lay down, right in the middle of the path. She slept again, going deeper and deeper as the nurse administered another drug into her arm.

Simpa watched as the nurse administered the drug. Deep inside, she wished it would let the leader pass into an infinite coma. She did not want her to pass on. That would be too good.

"She must be having very intense dreams," the nurse said to Simpa. "Usually when a person is in this state, they are very calm. I am giving the sedative an extra boost since she is so restless. She must have a lot on her mind."

Simpa just smiled, feigning sympathy at the nurse.

"Now, I can put my plan into place. It is time for justice!" Simpa thought to herself.

They set the ceremony for two days later. Simpa's dream had never been this grand, but here it was, in real life.

"As Executive Aide and highest-ranking officer in the leader's team, I accept the position of Interim Leader. I take great pride in accepting this office until such time as She is fit to return or there is a need for an election," she said as she spoke to the thousands of people before her.

No one challenged her accepting the duties of the leader. After all, it was stated in the documents of the office that She held this trust in Simpa, in the possibility of her incapacitation.

Now, these infidels were going to pay!

Chapter 32

Simpa hardly slept that night. She was now She! The most powerful person in this country. She knew she was the right person for this job. The world would know She has come to town!

The next morning, Simpa found herself seated at her new desk two hours earlier than anyone else. She was ready to tackle the affairs of the country. It can't be that difficult of a job, if her former boss could do it.

There was a stack of papers on the desk looking like they needed to be attended to. As She tore into them, her face went pale.

"What does this mean? Who do these people think they are? We are the greatest nation that has ever existed! How can they threaten us with war if we do not pay up our loan in full?"

"You have thirty days to pay us back or we are going to take over your country," was all She heard on the other end of the phone, followed by a very noisy click.

"It is no wonder she wanted to excite the natives, and then when that didn't work, she tried to shut down the mill and that town. This country is screwed!

I am Superwoman though, and I have thirty days to figure this out," She told herself.

Calling in her Minister of Finance, She was ready to settle this problem.

"Just print some more paper money and sell them to other unsuspecting countries. That should do the trick," was her first thought. "Let's see what this joker has to say."

As he walked in the door, she was pulling up the bank records on the computer. She had him close the curtains, so they had privacy, then showed them on the big screen TV so they could both see.

It took little effort to see the country was in dire straits. By the end of the meeting with the Minister, Simpa was already regretting having taken the job on. The glory gone, replaced by a very stained, empty tin can. Her beloved country was broke.

The question now in her mind that begged to be answered was what had happened to the money? Sure, that nasty business with that orb a while back had cost a bundle, but the country seemed to have bounced back.

She continued searching through the financial records on the computer, clicking open each file, then closing it. She was almost falling asleep; it was such a tedious job to her. She was just about to close out the folder when she noticed a file hidden by a wall inside the former leader's own private section. Trying to open it, all she got were warnings from the computer's security system. After the third attempt, she found the Chief of Computer Security standing at her door. He was not a happy camper!

"What are you doing, Madame? The alarm bells are driving everyone crazy," he said as he pushed her and her chair out of the way. It took him only a minute to return everything to normal.

"You cannot access that file," he said to her in a very stern voice.

"What do you mean?" She yelled back at him. "I am the leader of this country. There is nothing, and I mean nothing, that I cannot do or have. Now open this file right now! Your job is on the line!"

She was beside herself with anger. The insolence of this man!

As she attempted to regain control of the computer, the Minister approached from behind her. He said in a muted tone, "You cannot fire me. I do not work for you."

Turning to face him, her face was full of rage. She was going to show this person who was the boss. She was going to throw him out of the building herself!

"We had just finished retraining the former leader when she took ill. It is inconvenient that we now have to retrain you," the Chief of Computer Security said as he stepped right up to her side. She felt a pinch in her arm.

"We have no time to waste," were the last words she heard.

Reverend Harry, Rose, and the Wind Surfers sat in the board room at the center. If there ever was a time for feeling sullen, this was it.

"Our country is in a fine mess. I wish we could just wave a magic wand and make things right. Why do humans have to create such messes? Don't they understand we are supposed to work together to make things better for everyone?" muttered Harry.

As fast as the words fell out of his mouth, their favorite angel was on site. Rachel smiled, then said, "It does seem humans feel a strong need to live in discord, choosing chaos over peace and strength seems to have become the chosen line of expression. If they would learn from the chaos, there could be some benefit.

Instead, the masses choose to believe they create power from the chaos, so they keep making disruptions. This provides them with the opportunity to take advantage of others until the chaos reaches a breaking point.

We must just sit and let this scene play out, even if it seems to be extreme. The players must continue until they learn, or they find their lives incapacitated in some way. After all, it is a universal truth that choices have consequences.

To wave my magic wand over this situation may end this learning event. It would just bubble up at another time. We must sit to the side and continue to monitor the progression of events... and trust."

That was some powerful injection Simpa received! She woke up sometime later to unfamiliar surroundings. What was she doing out in this forest? What were these clothes she was wearing? These are not Armani!

She looked around, trying her best to understand what had occurred. At first, she thought she was by herself, but as her awareness expanded, she realized... she was in the scene she had dreamed of when she was in a coma after her accident at the mill.

"What am I doing here?" she cried to herself. "I hate being outside. I want to go back to my nice, friendly city."

"Come on you. Let's get moving. We have a nice new job for you up ahead." With that, the man who spoke to her pulled her to her feet with the rope that bound her wrists.

She almost fainted again as she realized this was the same dream. However, now she was one of the enslaved. The rope around her waist tightened as the other captives trudged forward. He said to her, "Next time you try to take over my job, you will lose more than your freedom! You will fetch a pretty penny now. A little bonus for us at the market!"

"We will change leaders when I say. This woman has been a nuisance for far too long," he said to the Minister of Finance. "Who does she think she is, upsetting our carefully crafted plans?

We already have control over the finances of that other country without their knowledge, and soon we will have this one. That will make us the richest people on the planet. No one will be able to stop us!"

"I agree with you, my friend. It is too bad they could not figure this out themselves. Once we merge them together, we will create legislation to eliminate personal freedoms. Then they will have to do what we say, or die!" said the minister through his now well-practiced evil grin.

"What shall we do about a leader, though? We need a puppet in place to be the fall guy when this all happens," the leader questioned.

"Let's just leave the curtains closed for now and not make any announcements about this one falling ill. Maybe we can move our schedule ahead with the merger. We just need a little war as a cover," the other man said.

———————————————

Simpa continued in her dream, resentful of being added to the slave list. She had to do something about this. After all, she was not slave material!

It was still a long walk to their destination, so she played along while she thought up a plan.

It was cold, sleeping on the ground that night, so sleep evaded her. However, her mind was busy churning away. Late in the night, she had a visitor.

Rachel smiled and spoke in a whisper in her ear.

"I am Rachel. I serve the Universal God that created this earth and all that exists. I invite you to join me in this moment of knowing yourself through the eyes of God."

This time Simpa listened. She knew she was in a fix and just could not figure a way out. Maybe this pesky angel knew something that would help her.

"My dearest one, resistance to your own truth is your greatest challenge. You have a wonderful destiny, if only you could diffuse your need for control. It serves only to keep you in your own prison."

Simpa felt her ego boil at the suggestion that she interpreted as being full of herself. This was survival. She was a survivor.

"Should you continue letting your ego best you, your future will be fraught with a never-ending cycle of struggle. A cycle you cannot win. I invite you now to take a deep breath and let go. Let yourself become one with your higher truth. Let the vibration of the Universal God open your eyes to the glory of self-knowledge.

This offer I place before you is your only path to escape from your current destiny. I leave you to make the choice."

Simpa fell into a deep sleep, woken only by a stick poking her in the ribs sometime later.

"Come on you. Eat your mush and let's get on our way," the man spoke to her, in a voice that reminded her right away of the predicament she found herself in.

This day was just a repeat of the day before, and the day before that. Simpa knew they were getting close to the town where her current destiny lie. It was not a destiny of her choice. She understood from this dream that it was of her making.

As she walked, she thought about the words of the angel. She felt a great deal of resistance toward even thinking about her words. Throughout the day, the battle raged inside her.

Her mind knew it could be free without giving in. It was all-powerful!

And yet, there was this niggly little part somewhere in the back reaches of that mind of hers, that said listen to the angel.

That night, on the hard ground, Simpa wrestled with herself again. Rachel watched from above, saying nothing. Simpa could see her smiling that irresistible smile.

Her ego let go. Who could resist that smile? Simpa melted into a pile of tears.

As they walked the next day, an odd thing occurred. They were walking along as usual, when the horses all decided at once to take a break. There was nothing their masters (so the humans thought) could do as the horses lay down to take a break.

Without a second thought, Simpa and the other would be slaves took their leave.

"Freedom at last," Simpa thought as she ran into the forest. "Just find somewhere to hide for now."

As they gathered in the cave, Simpa took over the situation. After all, she was a born leader, so she knew best. The others knew she had been one of their captors though, so when she tried to organize them in her old, habitual way, all she got were looks of disdain and contempt. That was when the light came on.

Simpa took a deep breath, accepting her new life. A life with an angel. Simpa's body rattled with nervousness.

As she accepted her new life, she realized a young girl was speaking to the group. She did not know this girl. Where could she have come from? There were no villages near here, and why would a young girl be out here in the wilderness on her own?.

She took a deep breath, quieting her mind. She listened to the girl as she spoke.

"Close your eyes as you sit. Focus on your breath and let it calm you as you draw your breath in. Hold. Let your breath release. Hold. Keep following this pattern, then remain quiet and passive."

Simpa let go and followed the girl's simple instructions. She felt a freedom, a feeling she was unfamiliar with. She liked it. Her huge ego melted as she accepted her new life.

———————————————

Chapter 33

The country was in turmoil. War was looming. Fear was gripping the very soul of their existence. The Finance Minister and his partner were ecstatic! Everything was going to plan. It would not be very long now. They would be the richest people in the world.

With the country in chaos, no one would pay attention to the men, so they could now unlock that secured file folder. With this move, they would be unstoppable.

As the country prepared for war, the government initiated plans for a draught. Every person over the age of eighteen would take part. They would need everyone to prevent their country from being destroyed.

"Wow! That was some drug those guys had injected into me," Simpa said to herself. It felt like forever, but she did not know how long she had been out. Simpa looked around. She was not familiar with her surroundings. It was not a very nice place. It seemed obvious they thought she might die, so they had just dumped her out of the way.

Even though she was starving and filthy from her long sleep, she felt a determination inside her that would not be quelled. It was dark inside this place. So dark she could not even tell if it was inside a building or?

She stood up, being careful. She felt woozy, so she shuffled her feet forward to make sure each step kept her safe. It took only a few steps for her to find a wall. It was composed of earth. She turned in the opposite direction and repeated the process until she felt another wall: Gyproc.

It took only another minute for her to finish her explorations, then she sat back on the floor. "What kind of room would have three earthen walls and one manmade wall?" she asked herself.

Then the light went on! "Of course, this is a root cellar. There must be a building up above. There must also be access from the ceiling, since there were none on the walls!"

A new level of hope emerged in Simpa's mind. Stretching her arm upward as far as possible, she reached up to see if she could touch the ceiling. She had to jump, but she could touch it.

She then reasoned that since there was no door on any of the walls, there had to be a folding staircase in the ceiling. It would be near the manmade wall, so she shuffled over to investigate. It was easy to find the stairs, as it hung much lower than the ceiling. She still had to jump, but she grasped the upper edge of it. Down it came!

She climbed up the stairs until she reached the ceiling. With a little push, she was free!

"A barn," she thought. "That means they took somewhere me out in the country. I wonder if there is any food here. I am starving!"

"Who are you?" Simpa heard as she stepped outside. "Why are you inside my barn?" the man asked.

Simpa stared at him without answering, then she fainted.

The staff at the hospital were great. As Simpa woke up, she found herself lying in a comfy hospital bed in a private room. Outside the door, she could see a police officer standing outside.

"On your arrival, we searched you, but you had no identification on your person. The emergency staff decided to just leave you on a gurney in the hallway in emergency. However, the man who found you told us what he knew, so we were suspicious.

When the police arrived, they recognized you at once, so we moved you into this room. If you are up to it, we are making a meal for you, then the detective would like to speak with you. Okay?" The nurse smiled as she spoke.

Simpa relaxed and agreed. She was ready for some solid food.

"Madame leader," said the detective as he entered. "I am with the federal police force. I have been assigned to your case. We have placed the highest security level possible on this situation, as we feel there may be a national threat involved.

With the current situation of the country being close to war, we feel your situation might be related."

Simpa did not know about the increase in tension between the two countries. Many events have occurred since her last conscious memory. She was about to be updated.

Simpa told her version of the events as she recalled, leaving out the part that she had altered the paperwork regarding her dismissal. Her focus was about the meeting with the Minister of Finance, and the other man, who claimed to be head of Computer Security.

The detective listened and made notes. He had heard rumors there were problems at the top of the government, but the order had come down that no one was to investigate, as the issues were beyond the clearance levels of any of the police. These circumstances had now changed the rules.

With this additional information, the police expanded their investigation. Many questions needed to be answered!

What was behind that wall in the computer?

Who else was involved?

Was there a reason the former leader was still unconscious?

These were the questions at the top of the list. They knew they would need to be careful and sneaky, or the investigation would be foiled.

Simpa only received minor injuries during the ordeal. However, the effects of the drug and the fact that she had not eaten, for what turned out to be a week, had left her in a weakened state. No one would even hear of her leaving her bed until she felt better, no matter the situation outside the walls of the hospital.

Simpa slept. She dreamed. Guess who came to visit?

"I am Rachel. I serve the Universal God that created this earth and all that exists. I invite you to join me in this moment of knowing yourself through the eyes of God."

Rachel remained quiet, just smiling at this poor, tormented person. She wondered if she had reached the limits of her ego. Would she give in to her heart?

Simpa lay there, staring at the woman in her dream. She recalled being very nasty to the woman once before, sending her off. Simpa felt exhausted, having fought the battle of her lifetime. She realized the battle needed to end.

"I do not know what you want of me. However, your presence is welcome. I am tired and cannot fight any longer. What do you want?"

"My blessed child, you have lived once again when your enemies believed they have defeated you. Your strength is admirable. You need your strength for the times that are upon your nation.

I wish to assist you in stepping into your strength at this time by helping you to be even stronger. I wish you to become a champion of your people and to make a permanent positive mark in the history of your country."

Simpa listened. She was too tired to fight anymore. She could feel a stirring in her being, one she was unfamiliar with.

"As you lay here, let yourself move into your being. Be still. Let your mind relax. You are safe. Let the thoughts and feelings you feel wash away. Embrace the quiet. Pay attention to your breath. As thoughts and feelings come up distracting you, refocus on your breath until you feel calm and one with yourself."

Rachel returned to the vapor, leaving Simpa to dream, but her instructions stayed in her mind. Simpa felt so tired from this ordeal, she complied with the instructions.

"What is this feeling? I have never felt so relaxed in my entire life. I think I will like this," Simpa said to herself.

She had nothing else to do since the police did not allow any visitors. Her mind liked to be busy, and since nothing else was pressing, she continued focusing on her breath, relaxing.

Later in the day, Rachel returned. It was almost a race who would smile at the other first!

"My dearest Simpa, you have achieved the most precious blessing, that of returning to your heart. Do you recall having achieved this feeling once before?"

Simpa's mind searched for a moment. Then she recalled. "The little girl in the cave, in my dream," she replied. "She taught the group of us who were escaping the people on the horses how to do that same exercise."

Rachel smiled.

"Now it is time for you to use this tool to help yourself become all you can express. Are you ready? Are you ready to accept your true destiny?"

As Simpa opened her eyes while she lay in bed, she could feel her entire being shift. Yes, she was ready to accept her true destiny. She now understood that depending on her mind alone was exhausting and worse, too limiting!

The feeling in her body became more intense. It felt so good. Soon she felt like she was glowing. Her energy returned. Her love of life returned.

As she watched, Simpa let herself accept her new life. Rachel waved her hand in a slow rhythmic pattern over Simpa as she lay there. Soon, she could see the dark energy of old dysfunctional beliefs evaporating into the Universe. Rachel knew this process would take many sessions to attain the level of clarity needed for this person to achieve her life purpose. And a grand one it was!

Since time was of the essence, considering the situation percolating outside her door, Simpa dove into the healing process. She knew it was up to her to save her country. Rachel smiled as she watched the evolution unfold before her.

———————————

The door opened. Simpa expected it was a nurse coming to bring her lunch or some medicine. It was not.

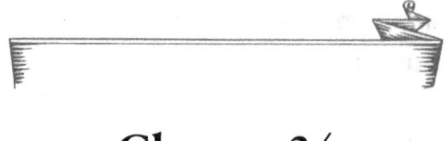

Chapter 34

Simpa thought she was still in a dream state as the woman entered her room. Her feelings of fear jumped into action for about a second.

There was something about this woman. She radiated love in every cell of her body. There was something familiar about this woman. She knew she had never met her before, and yet she knew her.

The woman sat down on the edge of the bed. Taking Simpa's hand in the most gentle, loving way, she smiled. Simpa fainted.

As she slipped into a dream state, she returned to the cave, realizing the woman holding her hand at present was the same person as the little girl who had led the group in the breathing exercise.

When she returned to the outer world, she found Merle still holding her hand.

"Welcome to your new life, my friend. I am here to assist you in any way I can. We have a lot of work to do to save our country," Merle said as she smiled at her.

Simpa sat right up and pulled her new friend into a big hug.

It was not long, and Simpa was ready to tackle the situation outside the hospital. Almost a month had passed since she had sat in the leader's seat. This meant war was on the horizon.

She wanted to check in with the police to find out how the investigation was going, but there was something far more important to attend to right now.

Simpa needed to stop this pending war. She knew it only served the two men. Nobody else wanted the fight. She needed to get to the other country and speak with their leader, but how?

Merle just smiled as Simpa pondered the situation. Without Simpa noticing, Merle took her hand. In less than the heartbeat of a butterfly, Simpa stood in the lobby of the capitol building... of the other country.

She was alone. Time was of the essence, so she did not ponder the situation for long. She needed to get to see the leader, and quick.

However, she had gotten to this building, it was pretty smart. She had landed past security, so that was one obstacle out of the way. She stood in a lobby. Seeing several comfy-looking chairs, she felt it would be of benefit to collect herself before she made her next move.

Sitting down, Simpa moved into meditation. She was getting good at this meditation thing now, so once she achieved the desired level of connection, she visualized sitting with this leader, then saw herself shaking hands with the leader and sharing a hug. When she felt she had manifested the desired result in the visualization, she took a deep breath, then opened her eyes.

A few moments later, the door to an elevator opened into the lobby. Out walked the leader and her entourage. They appeared not to be in a hurry, as they all gathered in the area before Simpa, chatting and laughing. Simpa stood, hoping the leader would recognize her.

She heard the leader say to the group, "We are in control of this event, so do not worry. If these people want war, it is us that have to push the button."

It was then that the leader recognized Simpa standing a few feet away. The leader looked like she was seeing a ghost. At first, she said nothing at first but stood there staring in disbelief.

Simpa smiled at the leader, hoping she would speak to her.

The entourage went quiet as they looked at Simpa. Then they looked back at the leader. The quiet seemed to last for an eternity. It was a good thing no one had a pin to drop. It would have sounded like an explosion.

The leader walked over to Simpa. She was a very diplomatic person, well experienced in the world of politics. However, it is quite unusual for the leader of another country to be standing in the lobby of their building, with no appointment or other notification of their pending arrival. This is especially true when it is the leader of a country which one might be at war with at any moment from now.

To maintain her power in the situation, the leader shook Simpa's hand, then invited her to sit down again... and wait. She said she would be back in a couple of hours. She had an important engagement to attend to.

At first, Simpa fell back into her old personality. Catching herself, she closed her eyes, focusing on her breath. She visualized sitting down with the leader, having a pleasant conversation. She saw herself shaking hands with the leader like they had reached an agreement.

The leader got about fifty feet away when she stopped. She sent an aide back to speak with Simpa.

"Would you like to join us for lunch, Madame?" the aide said.

There was no business spoken at lunch, by the leader's order. It was a standard rule of business. There was enough time for business talk later. Simpa could not sit still. She felt eager to speak to the leader, but she respected the rule.

One of Simpa's new habits since embracing this new life was to bless her food. As they placed it in front of her, she placed her hands over the dish. She closed her eyes as she gave thanks. When she opened her eyes, she realized the entire group was doing the same thing. The only ice left in that gathering was in people's drinks!

The leader sat across from Simpa. Her smile reminded her of Rachel's... and Merle's. Hmmm!

Back in the leader's office a long while later, Simpa sat. They did not sit across the desk from each other as she had expected. They sat nearby in a space that would remind one of their home living room. She was not alone. Several of her lunch buddies sat down to take part in the conversation.

"It took aback us when we saw you standing in the lobby, Simpa. Even this shock was trumped when we realized the borders between our countries are closed, even to political leaders.

Can you... how did you get here?" the leader exclaimed.

"I do not know," Simpa replied. "I was meditating and visualizing meeting with you. When I opened my eyes, I was sitting in your lobby.

My life has changed so much in recent days. I gave up being the angry, determined person I had been for so many years. I made the choice to live in the energy of Universal Love. Now new things happen so often that I just cannot explain... like showing up here today."

The leader smiled at her, saying nothing at first.

"I had heard you had died. The Finance Minister proclaimed himself as interim leader. As soon as he did, he began preparing the country for war. Is he still leader, then?"

"Yes, he does not even know I am alive. When the people found me and took me to the hospital, they placed me in the highest priority security. They even had a guard outside my door, so no one could visit.

Because of the tenuous situation between our countries, when they released me, I felt it paramount that we speak before announcing myself to the world. I do not support any kind of war with anyone."

Another pin could have dropped in the room as it went quiet again for several minutes. The leader was just about to ask another question when Simpa continued.

"The police have been able to determine the Finance Minister and the head of Computer Security are up to something. As interim leader, I only had a little time to make any investigation of my own. I found a hidden file on my computer. When I tried to open it, an alarm went off and the head of security was right there.

The next thing I knew I was lying in a dark root cellar, left for dead."

Again, the room remained quiet. This was a lot for anyone to absorb.

"I remained in the hospital for this past month. I have had no outside communication with the world, so I do not know how things have progressed. I just know I want to stop this situation before anyone regrets it.

I also want to find out what these men are up to."

Chapter 35

"What do you mean, there is going to be no war?" the finance minister said to his aide.

This person had become quite irritating, as leaders sometimes do, since they think they are next in line to God, so they don't have to be polite.

The aide said again, "We have received a notice from the other guys. They will not invade our country. They wish to work things out peacefully."

"Get out of my office!" he yelled at the aide. Picking up the phone, he called the Head of Computer Security.

"Get up here right now. We have a big problem."

This decision had messed up his plans. They needed a war so they could cover up their plan. Someone was sure to notice if they did not have some other major activity to misdirect people's eyes.

"We have already tried and failed twice to cause an insurrection. Now, these guys don't want to go to war with us! What are we supposed to do now?" he yelled at the other man.

"Let's declare war on them instead. We can say they have humiliated us, and we need to show them our strength," said the chief.

So the scene was now set. A war would ensue. Even if they had to start it themselves, they were going to have a war.

They sent notices to the military to be prepared. Recruiters were notified to increase the ranks.

"Get those people into uniforms asap, for the sake of freedom in our country," was the rally cry.

The recruiters reached out. They set up temporary offices in every town. Pretty posters showing how wonderful people would look in their uniforms were plastered on billboards and poles throughout the country. Other posters elicited excitement about doing their patriotic duty.

However...

This was the same country where Reverend Harry and his now very large ensemble lived.

And, if you recall, we asked earlier "What would happen if a country declared war, and no one showed up to play?"

Well, it happened once. And now it was happening again. Nobody showed up.

All those wonderful posters did no good. The recruiting offices were empty. Truth be told, even the recruiters were only doing it for the extra pay.

After a week of no one showing up, the men were livid, to say the least.

"We will have to go with the existing army," said the Finance Minister.

"Can't," was all that was uttered by the aide, who stood across the desk from him.

"What do you mean, can't?" he said in a most impolite tone.

"They did not come back from their raid at the mill," he replied.

The man gulped. His blood pressure was about to reach a record high.

"Then I guess we will have to make it a police action. Call out our SWAT team."

"Can't."

"Do you know any other words? What do you mean, can't?"

The minister was now beyond himself with anger. His blood pressure reached another new high.

"The mill," was all the aide said.

"Find some other people in other towns and force them into uniforms. We need to get this war going before they invade us," he yelled at the aide again.

"Can't," was all he heard again.

Everything has its limits. The Minister's blood pressure was about to reach that level. He waved his hand in expectation at the aide.

"They were all grateful for the uniforms, but they said they were not interested in playing war. They said they needed to attend their yoga classes."

The minister groaned and pounded his head again and again on the top of the desk.

––––––––––––––––––

"No matter what happens in the near future, we are going to have a war. Our plan depends on it," the minister mumbled to the Chief.

"I guess we will have to do it ourselves then, since no one else will show up. Without an army or a police force, we have no way to force the people to comply," said the Chief.

Without another thought, the two men headed out of the office. They were going to be the army!

Time was of the essence, so they did not even slow down as they approached the security gate at the army camp. Breaking right through the wooden arm, pieces flew up into the air. Of course, causing damage to the car as they slammed down.

It was hard to continue driving with a smashed windshield, but no one in the car cared. They were on a mission now.

Like at the security gate, the entire camp was a ghost town. There was not a soul to be found.

After searching for a while, they found the vehicle compound.

"Let's find a big truck and hook a cannon to it. We will send them a message they will never forget!" sneered the Minister.

He ran up to a big truck. Grabbing the door handle, he turned and pulled. It was locked.

Flabbergasted, he stared in disbelief at the Chief.

It took him about twenty minutes to find the keys. He felt this day was becoming overfilled with challenges, but he was determined.

He jumped into the truck. The engine roared to life, then sputtered and died. Out of fuel!

Back in for another set of keys. He brought several this time. It took several more tries before he found a suitable truck... with fuel.

"Now let's find a cannon. One shot of that baby will show them who is boss!" They both laughed.

Never having been in the military, or having done any real work in their lives, they did not know how to hook the cannon to the big truck. A simple thirty-second job took fifteen minutes, and they still missed hooking up the safety chains! Boy, some people!

They were just about back outside the security gate when the Chief yelled, "Stop! We do not have any bullets for the cannon."

Cursing as loud as he could as he turned the truck back around, the Minister fumed. "Where would they store these things?"

Another hour and a large crowbar provided them with the required bullets for the cannon. (They did not know or even care they were not called bullets!)

Success! Now they were heading to the front. Since only a small mountain range divided the two countries, it would not be difficult to set themselves up. An excellent target was in sight.

They did not even care what they were going to use as a target, as long as it was something inside the other country. Even a farmer's barn would do the trick.

What they did not realize was that they were being observed the whole time they set this business up... by Merle.

She was having the time of her life, watching these characters. It quite surprised Merle at their tenacity. One would have thought the Minister might have had a stroke by now considering the level of his blood pressure. However, the two men continued on their campaign to show the world who was in charge.

They found a flat and wide ridge as they conquered the low mountain. They were now envisioning themselves as great military leaders as they attempted to set the cannon on point. Too bad backing up trailers was not in their skill set either.

After almost dumping the cannon and the attached truck over the edge, they had managed to park the vehicles in a position suitable for the job. The men struggled with their breath from the anticipation. Victory was on the rise!

Merle continued to observe as the men dragged the box with the "bullet" over to the back end of the cannon. They had watched enough war movies to know it did not get dropped into the hole at the front, so their tender egos got to cheer a bit.

It took a bit to figure out how to load it, but with only another dozen profanities, they achieved it. The cannon was now loaded. Then came setting the trajectory. (That is my word as they did not even know the word existed!)

"All set!" the Minister said in a very military voice. He pushed the Chief out of the way, so he could push the button himself.

Do you remember way back how Mike, Merle's male half, learned how to do that thing with his hands to create a positive force of energy to stop bad guys in their tracks?

Well, guess what?

It works on "bullets" too!

The Minister pushed the button, then covered his ears, expecting a loud bang like he had heard cannons on television produce. He was soooo excited!

There was a bang... sort of.

The cannon bounced back, knocking both men to the ground. As the bullet soared out of the barrel, it flew like the speed of... well, let's say it exited the cannon.

The bullet lay on the ground about six feet from the end of the barrel. The entire episode was about as dramatic as watching a camel spit at the local game farm.

"Again!" the Minister yelled.

This time, they saw the powder pack. Loading it into the appropriate spot in the cannon, they prepared for the big event.

The Minister pushed the button again, this time jumping out of the way, so he did not get knocked over again.

"What a beautiful sight!" they both thought as the bullet soared through the air... and melted. Its remains lay on the ground, a molten mass.

Merle felt pleased with herself.

They were glad they had brought as many of the bullets as they could lay their hands on. It took all of them, and more. By the time they had shot every bullet off, all they had achieved was creating a big puddle of molten lead about thirty feet away.

Both men wore sheepish grins. They were very relieved that no one had seen this whole episode. They could hang their heads in misery with no other person any the wiser.

Chapter 36

With the two men away from the office, the police officers made their entry. Now was the opportunity to get in and gain access to all the files, including the ones behind the hidden wall, with no interference.

This brief visit should not take very long since Simpa had told them about the secret compartment. With their own computer expert in hand, they were going to move the investigation to a new level this day.

Merle watched from above as the military action melted (just like the bullets). The men had run out of ammunition, and now their minds.

They stood at the front end of the cannon, looking into the barrel. It wreaked of action, but it now stood quiet, serving no more purpose than a screen door on a submarine.

The men slumped down on the ground. Their minds joined the molten mass on the ground before them, never to return.

Merle did not want the men to suffer more, so she sent a message to Simpa through her mind.

Simpa's visit with the leader of the other country had proven fruitful. They would initiate an investigation into their end of the situation. They both concluded that untoward activities had been occurring on both sides of the mountain.

After a delightful afternoon, Simpa pointed her car back to her country. As soon as she reached the border, she felt a niggly feeling. She needed to stop for a few minutes.

Knowing there was a rest stop ahead with a spectacular view overlooking her new friend's country, she turned off, heading up a side road. Guess what she found?

"Now you can put the investigation into high gear," Simpa told the chief investigator as she stood looking at the two unconscious men. "Nobody will stand in the way. Please contact your counterparts in the other country as they are investigating the matter from their end."

Sure enough, as one would expect, the hidden files did indeed contain photographs and other collectibles of the sort one would have if they wished to manipulate another's morals. It also contained draught papers for a new constitution that contravened the country's current personal freedom legislation.

Digging deeper, they found a file containing information about several secret bank accounts around the world. It was no wonder these men were determined to get the war started.

The investigation took a long time to complete, but since the leaders of both countries were now best friends, the perilous situation had evaporated into the ethers.

With the collectibles destroyed and the money returned to the appropriate bank accounts, everyone sighed in relief. Both countries were in fine financial shape.

They found the former leader through the investigation. She was living on a farm with some religious folks who had adopted her after they had found her wandering in the forest, claiming she was looking for mushrooms. They knew she would be a perfect member, since she did not know how to find those elusive fungi.

Once the investigators sat her down, she was glad to divulge what she knew.

"At last, I can clear my conscience! I have almost lost my mind from having to keep this whole nefarious affair a secret.

The Chief of Internet Security and the Finance Minister loved to host gigantic parties. Since they felt they were such important people, they did not let things like moral boundaries bother them much.

After they had held a few of these shindigs, the Chief realized there was a financial opportunity, so the money rolled in... after they had a hidden camera installed. It is amazing what people will do to protect themselves once the hand is caught in the cookie jar.

At first, the parties were exclusive to locals, but then they saw the need to expand. They did not care they were destroying the economies of both countries. As the parties got better and better, so did their ability to lock into money-making situations.

Since most of the birds caught in the cages had little of their own money, they became quite willing to be otherwise resourceful. Department budgets ran over like water over the falls!"

"What was the plan for all this money?" asked the investigator.

"The money was secondary. Power and control were the goals. They planned to turn our country into their private kingdom. No more elections, or other unnecessary stuff like personal freedom. Anything that would either cost them money or might be annoying to them was to be filtered out.

They had that machine created to interfere in the weather a few years ago. That took a lot of the money. Almost bankrupted them. They had become so absorbed in their mission by now, their lust had taken control.

Then that machine went crazy, and it took control. It thwarted their plans until it exploded. The men did not know what had happened to it, but they were glad it was gone.

They resumed the plan even though the country was close to bankruptcy, and they had no way to cover their tracks. However, no one else was any to the wiser, yet. The parties blossomed again, and the money rolled in, but the people from the government of the other country had realized what the men were doing. They wanted their money back, now that the economy had returned to normal.

A lot of heads rolled when the government investigated the causes of the budget overruns!

The men needed to cover up their activities by creating a diversion. That was when they started inciting the unrest with the indigenous people. When that fizzled, they went after that mill.

They were determined they were not giving back the money they had filtered into the secret bank accounts. They needed to create something as a cover. That is the last I knew. As you know, I suffered a severe breakdown. I woke up to find myself living here.

This whole sordid affair came to my attention only after they had perpetrated it. I was going to report it, but I got sick before I could."

The investigator realized she had recovered enough to create a story that worked well to cover her participation in the events, making it sound as if she had no part in the whole sordid affair. He let it go for the immediate time. He had a lot of loose ends to tie up for now.

The former leader was pleased with her little performance, smirking as she watched the investigators leave. It would only be a little while longer, then she could reward herself for all she had suffered... or so she thought.

That night, the former leader had a visitor in her dreams. At first, she thought she had slipped back into that terrible level of the mind only a coma can produce as Rachel spoke.

"*I am Rachel. I serve the Universal God that created this earth and all that exists. I invite you to join me in this moment of knowing yourself through the eyes of God.*"

Rachel smiled from overhead as she waited for her to respond. She remained still and quiet as the former leader stared at her.

It was several long minutes before she responded. "I do not know who you are or why you come to me in my dreams, but I have made my choices. I know myself and do not need you in my life."

And with that, she turned over and slipped off into another dream. Rachel hovered overhead, invisible to the woman as the dreams began.

She tossed and turned through the night, dreaming of horses misbehaving and the disappearance of the would-be slaves. It pleased her to no end as she dreamed of laughing at the people she had forced to do her bidding, even if they suffered in misery.

Then, late in the night, she saw the orb. She heard the music, the monotonous, hypnotic drum beats. She saw the drummers. They were so beautiful in their costumes. They played and played.

"What enchanting music," she said to herself. "I want to hear more."

Moving closer, inching nearer and nearer, past the lineup of children screaming as they suffered from hunger and upset from being separated from their parents. Deep inside, she knew she had caused their hurts. What did she care?

"Listen to the sound of the drums. There are more now. They are beating so fast! I just want to be closer to them."

Rachel faded away, knowing that freedom of choice still reigned supreme in the Universe.

In the morning, when she did not appear for breakfast, one lady came in to her room to check on her, only to find an empty bed.

It had not been a dream!

Chapter 37

L ife back at Greenwood Commons carried on in a blissful state. It was springtime now, so the spring stock of new plants shone their little heads out from their beds of soil. Snowdrops and crocuses smiled everywhere as the sun shone down on another glorious day.

All the members of the complex were outside walking around, enjoying the start of new life in the gardens, pushing their hands deep into the soil to feel the wonderful vibrations of life that Mother Earth manifested in such abundance.

Even the children took part as they stood before their box gardens. Their recent dreams were not of candy and new dollies. No, they dreamed of the new veggies that would grow soon in these mini-gardens. They could already taste the snap peas fresh off the vine and little cherry tomatoes melting in their mouths!

There was so much to look forward to!

There was going to be new life in another form at Greenwood Commons as well. More construction!

The original concept of four buildings that Dawn had designed had already exploded into ten buildings. She smiled as she wandered throughout the massive estate as the spring weather took hold, letting the site show its maturity.

Everywhere she looked, everything fit. It all worked in congruence with Mother Earth's master plan.

It was going to be easy to expand the site for the next set of buildings. Greenwood Commons had become a village of its own, no longer just a cohousing site. It had expressed in a more comprehensive state. There was a main street with shops selling almost anything one could desire. Cafes with outside patios were everywhere, serving tasty drinks and treats. Life felt good.

As people sat outside enjoying themselves, they were treated to the fragrances of wonderful and tasty cooking herbs growing in planters near the light posts along the street. The little plants embraced their new lives, thrusting their beautiful aromas into the air.

It was now time for the biggest expansion yet. They had set a town hall meeting to create and start the next layer of growth for the area.

The mayor opened the discussion.

"It gives me great pleasure to host this meeting. We have the opportunity to work together to continue and expand the great work we have all done in our city over the recent years.

We have two fronts of opportunity to expand our vision. I think the biggest challenge is going to be holding onto the reins of our own excitement through the process.

At City Hall, we have watched and taken part in the growth of Greenwood Commons as it has expanded and matured into the fine village it now expresses. Everyone from the janitor and the clerks right through to the council is one hundred percent in support of the vision that sits before us.

In fact, my first presentation at this meeting today is a proposal to merge the balance of our fair town into the Greenwood Commons legal description. All the property owners who live outside of this property wish to merge into one collective property, adopting the philosophy of cohousing.

We propose City Hall become the central office. It will continue its role in dealing with the legalities of property management. We will also have a committee who will manage the ongoing affairs of maintaining and improving life in our fair town. We will also continue the duties of being the liaison with the federal government.

As mayor, I will maintain my role as general overseer of administration. However, I will not carry on as an individual decision maker. My role will be collaborative, as a member of a cohousing organization."

As he stopped to take a breath, all the people in the room stood, cheering and clapping. Dawn beamed as she heard her vision take another huge leap forward.

The leader of the Indigenous people now rose. Everyone took their seats expecting more great news.

"This indeed is going to be an exciting year for everyone, having observed the growth of Greenwood Commons since its birth. We have observed the lives of the members, and even took part in events with you. One question though. Where is that funky little band that seemed to appear a lot before? We have not seen them for a while!

Since Greenwood Commons has expanded so much from its original plan, our properties now border each other. We invoked the concept of ruling by consensus into our administration a while ago. The residents felt it was essential to their own growth to have more input into the affairs of the overall community.

Dawn has also worked with us to incorporate the philosophy of working in communion with nature into our land use designs. Many of the members have shared dreams where they recalled our ancestors living with this philosophy.

To celebrate our ancestors, we have implemented as many strategies of permaculture into our concepts as possible.

In most recent times, we have felt the urge to move to the next step to create a stronger, more vibrant community. We are all in agreement that we also merge our properties into the legal description of Greenwood Commons!

Every person at the meeting sat motionless as the Chief spoke. As she concluded her speech, the quiet continued. Everyone felt stunned.

The silence continued for quite some time. The Chief sat down and joined in the quiet. She could tell by the looks on the faces of the participants that this was a good quiet.

Dave sat with his mill people a few days after the announcements of the merger.

"We are in an unprecedented situation. To facilitate the manufacturing of all the wood we will need, we are going to have to make a dramatic increase in the acquisition of garbage plastics.

We are already collecting plastics from every known source in our country. We now will have to embark on an international collection program.

There is, however, an impending issue. Because we are a forward thinking company, we are organizing a think tank focused on revising the process we use for making our wood at present.

As we continue in our day-to-day work, if anyone has any ideas regarding new materials, please drop a message in the suggestions box so we can discuss it at the next meeting. Time is of the essence."

The mill buzzed like never before. It was very fortunate that all the police officers and the soldiers who had attended the parking lot breakfast stayed on to work at the mill. They needed their able bodies and minds as the mill expansion developed!

This developing situation concerned Dave. He felt stumped.

He knew himself well enough that when he felt this way, there was only one place to go.

"Well, Dave. It is high time we had a visit. Welcome." Rose was always pleased to see Dave. She knew there would be some exciting news. There would also be a puzzle to solve.

"We have an interesting situation developing, my friend. Before it becomes a problem, we need to find an answer.

It is with gratitude that the people have forced the petrochemical companies to replace plastic in the marketplace. The earth breathes much easier now. However, our mill relies on plastic waste as a component of the wood we make.

With the new buildings planned for Greenwood Commons, we are reaching out to international markets to collect whatever plastics we can garner. However, we know this is temporary. Our success in cleaning up the earth is now creating a problem.

I come to you today to ask if you will help us find the answer to this riddle."

As Dave and Rose sat meditating on the situation, nine of the seats at the table found themselves with people sitting on them. Not much later, Reverend Harry filled the tenth seat.

Harry looked at each of the Wind Surfers, smiling (more like smirking!) He said, "I still prefer the traditional way of entering a room!"

With a good laugh, they all joined in the meditation, connecting their consciences together in unison with Source.

Rachel then joined in. *"Wait for me!"* she laughed. *"It is nice that I can be so casual in our group now. We have worked together so well for so many years."*

And, for the first time, instead of staying up in her cloud, she sat on a chair, just like everybody else.

"Is there tea? I am very thirsty!" she laughed, as she waved her hand over the table.

"That's better!" She said as everyone sipped the fresh cups of tea that had just manifested before them.

"This is an interesting situation. It will require thinking outside the box to solve this one," Rose said.

"It is worthy of recognition that people, (smiling at Dave), have allowed themselves to be forward-thinking without limitations. This way, we have time to relax and manifest a solution before it rears its head up. We do not need to embellish our fears anymore. Kudos to all!" Rachel said, proud of the growth all these folks had made in their personal journeys.

Everyone knew it would take a while for solutions to develop in their minds. They needed to clear any limited thinking out of the way to allow a fresh answer to manifest.

A little voice peeped up. It was a good thing everyone was quiet from meditating, so they could hear this tiny person. "I keep seeing pictures of that orb. At first, I tried to push the pictures away, but the pictures keep coming back into the screen of my mind." Papi said in as loud a voice as she could muster.

Rachel laughed as she recalled, *"Remember when we locked the orb in that capsule? They instructed us to not terminate it, as it would have a purpose sometime in the future."*

Harry jumped in then. "See, when we listen and trust, there is always an answer. And sometimes the answer is a concept that is much loftier than the human mind can conceive. Good going, Papi!"

They all returned to their meditations, waiting for the next step to be revealed.

Now it was Goose's turn. "We can drill and place two pipes right into the orb. It can turn all that negative energy it produces into a positive resource."

Then it was Condor's turn, as he gripped Hummingbird's shoulder to keep him in his chair. "We can, at last, get rid of garbage dumps! We collect all the garbage, then dump it into the downpipe."

Hummingbird getting loose of Condor's grip, blasted out of his chair, flipping into the air, doing somersaults as he yelled, "And the other pipe flows to the mill to produce the liquid needed to make the wood!"

Dave sat there, stunned, as he watched Hummingbird flitting about above the table. If that was not enough, Papi transitioned into her butterfly and joined him. Songbird, tweeting like crazy, followed behind.

Dave laughed as he watched the foray. "I knew we would find a brilliant solution! I must admit, though, I have never seen such a display of unbridled enthusiasm!"

Chapter 38

Now that things are getting sorted out all over the place, we can focus on pulling our story together.

Contentment was everywhere. Even the orb was feeling useful again. The mill roared to life as the nefarious free gift provided by the government people found its new position on the green chain, .

The mill now only needed a few people to operate it. In fact, more people were working in administration in the mill office than on the floor. Did this create an additional problem?

Nope! Fewer workers meant more people were available for other projects!

When the mill was first created, the employee benefits program included shares in the business for all employees. Now that they needed fewer people to operate the mill, they instituted job sharing. Each employee could now work one day per week... and receive equivalent to a full week's pay! How is that?

The mill management hired a consultant to help the employees explore ways to express their lives in constructive and beneficial ways. Many employees created businesses of their own. The common themes of these businesses were in specialized construction, environmental rehabilitation, or personal development workshops. And of course, more yoga studios!

Since the employees all had a steady paycheck, it would not be hard to get financing for their ventures. However, the bank also set up an investment bank that invested in each of the businesses.

The days of the hard luck farmers were gone! Mother Nature responded so well to the improvements in her earth that the ground gushed with beautiful plants. Many of the farmers also added commercial fish ponds to their venues to provide lighter protein for their diet.

The only regular farm animals to be found were dairy cows and goats. They bounded about in the fields instead of the old way of hanging out, feeling useless in a barn. The milk they produced was so yummy! Oh, and that cheese! Yum!

In fact, the cows and goats enjoyed being out in the fields that the farmers set up picnic tables near them so the locals could picnic as they watched the antics of these blessed animals. Who knew these animals could create their own games?

Was everything wonderful at the end of all the work that people had done? Was there peace ever after, or even anything close to something like peace on earth?

Well, in the newly expanded Greenwood Commons, life was the best ever.

Sometimes, people did not know how to deal with a stressful or challenging emotional situation, but they never amounted to anything because if the person having the issue did not know how to reframe the situation, a hundred others did.

They had also learned not to react to the situation when another was in over their head. They just provided support as the individual worked it out.

It is amazing how amazing life can be when everyone maintains a positive, open mind. The additional levels of resources available through direct connection with Source kept creativity at an all-time high. And since everyone had a steady income, the creativity found a new high as more resources became available.

––––––––––––––

So what about our government people? When we visited them last, the chief of security and the finance minister had meltdowns, the former leader went to visit the orb... permanently, and Simpa...

They ended the police investigation when they disclosed the information in the secret compartment in the computer. They destroyed all the information used to bribe other government officials.

The economies of both countries flushed with life when the absconded money found its way back where it belonged.

Since the investigation had made no mention of Simpa, she was excluded.

Having the three main characters who they suspected perpetrated the crimes, now removed from any place of importance, there was no value in continuing the investigation.

Now, having developed a solid relationship with Merle and Rachel, Simpa let her past life of always needing approval and control melt away. Her new focus was... yoga!

Simpa found her own inner happiness as the old, dysfunctional beliefs faded away. In time, she became an advocate for political change in the federal government.

In her mind, the old, archaic method of electing people who were unfit to hold a most prestigious position through lying and manipulation of voting streams needed to go, and she chose to do something to help it along its way.

She directed all her energy toward making positive change as she worked on her newfound focus. It was easy to get people to join forces with her. After all, the yoga centers had spread all over the country. In some cities, every church had become a yoga center. The exploding popularity of yoga meant a lot of people who were excited about the concept of change in the government processes.

There was some resistance as Simpa made regular speeches about her proposed vision of a new government. The resistance came from the big corporations.

As Simpa and her fellows gained popularity, the big guns pushed back. Even though the new lifestyle choices of the masses curtailed their power, they still held onto much of the financial power in the country.

They spent more time in meetings with their lawyers fighting this new wave of functional government that was more lean and healthy. In the end, the big corporations mounted class action lawsuits against Simpa's political organization. If they could not defeat her in the polls, they were going to muffle her in the courts.

Well, this all sounded like the best path for them, except...

Many of the judges and even the government employees were now also practicing yoga at the centers.

In the meantime, the investors at the bank had instituted a funding program for individuals investing in large corporations.

They knew their investment was going to be counterproductive for the short term. However; the goal was to break up any major shareholders in all these nefarious organizations. There was no intent in destroying the companies. Removing the power from the major stakeholders was the primary aim of the new plan. The big guys soon took up new hobbies.

It was not long in the scale of time that every large corporation changed its focus from being predators to focusing on serving the peoples' needs.

They invested more money in healthier medicines that helped people in their healing processes with better manufacturing practices on every level, and more environmentally supportive products.

Automobile manufacturers adapted their manufacturing to meet the increased demands for solar powered cars, electric scooters and bicycles.

They did not run very fast, but then, no one was in a hurry, anyway.

Speaking of electric power, a system of creating electricity became clear. The power generated through the orb soon lit up the entire country as it chewed up the garbage. The orb was the happiest and most miserable entity on the planet!

They removed all the power dams in the country to allow the rivers to flow as Mother Nature had designed. This created more fertile land for farming and land preservation.

The form of elections known for hundreds of years as first past the post now had become archaic. They recreated the government electoral process to provide accurate representation for the people.

The next step was creating an election committee, created and overseen by the people. Its job was to determine the fitness of any applicants who wished to serve as elected officials. They soon saw through any funny business and dealt with it!

All decisions about government policy were now discussed in committees comprising elected officials who had experience in that committee's area of focus.

Their purpose was to determine the most applicable and holistic method of improving current standards for the benefit of all... and Mother Earth for now and the long term.

The overall leader's job was now as a convener.

This person was to manage the infrastructure and communication systems between the committees, making sure everything went according to the new rules.

Not to leave out the employees of the government themselves, they went through a radical evolution as well.

Employees in the government offices now felt heard, so they could incorporate and support the new policies as they unfolded. They learned to like their jobs and now spent more time working in their jobs than ruminating at the local coffee shops.

The old way of running bureaucracies disappeared. They disallowed power pyramids at any level. Managers discovered their jobs were far more satisfying when they let go of the need to control, instead becoming facilitators supporting the growth and well-being of their fellow employees.

Rachel sighed as she looked down at her beloved children. They had now achieved a high level of growth in their lives. Was life on earth perfect?

No.

Why?

The Wind Surfers stood on the stage waiting to turn this crowd of millions into crazy dancing folks. The crowd was so large that, even from the vantage point of this high stage, they could not see the edges of the gathering in any direction.

They could feel the love directed at them from the folks as they readied to play. But first, Rachel would speak. As she appeared before them, the crowd became still. They knew and loved this Angel.

Rachel appeared at the front of the stage. Her golden hair flowing like a waterfall down her back over her favorite lavender floor-length gown. Her smiled radiated so much love, it competed with the sun shining in the sky.

"My beloved children. It gives me so much pleasure to be with you today as we celebrate and commemorate this new life that has begun.

We embrace this new life, not by forgetting the past and its traumas. We embrace this life by embracing the actions of rewriting our pasts. By taking the emotions out of those past hurtful situations, we dissolve the straight jackets we wore that claimed to keep us safe, that, in fact, kept us prisoners.

Through the power of love, love for ourselves, for the people around us and, especially, for the people whom we felt perpetrated these hurts, we now have reclaimed our truth, and our natural connection with Source.

As we have now discovered, many of the demands we placed on Mother Earth and her bounty of resources are no longer necessary. Being clear minded and in tune with the Cosmic, we have released our obsession to build fortresses around ourselves for protection. We now live as open vessels, connecting and communing with all.

We have realized that finding comfort with one's self has reduced illness and injury to the point of near extinction. Violence and crime are distant memories.

Love is the only energy that flows through our veins. Through love, we know the safety that God created in our natural design.

Are we finished now? Is there more?

My children, this is only the beginning!

Now, we can take a deep breath... and begin to evolve!

And, at that, Rachel turned to the Wind Surfers and yelled,

Hit it Gang!

About the Author

Monty has long had a passion for the esoteric world. Being a member of The Rosicrucian Order AMORC since 1981, he has been able to develop a good knowledge base, both theoretical and practical of both the mundane and esoteric worlds.

Monty's books are manifested through his resulting skill as a channeler and intuitive healer,

Monty's interest in the non-physical side of healing back in 1970 through a college program called Human Development. It was offered by two very open minded social workers. It was the beginning of his never ending quest to understand the human mind and its impact on people's lives from an intuitive perspective.

Monty is also a seasoned public speaker having been an active member of Toastmasters International, where he wrote and facilitated many workshops and keynote talks. In fact, his love for writing books came from creating his speeches in Toastmasters.

Monty's life passions are human evolution, nature and traveling. He has traveled to over 14 countries in his life including most of Canada and the US.

Monty favorite journey was walking the Camino Frances Trail (all 500 miles!) in Spain in both 2015 and 2017. He says he still has at least one more in him!

Monty's Books (so far!)
Available through all online book stores
Embracing The Blend
What Mom and Dad Didn't Know They Were Teaching You

Description: Understanding how your beliefs run your life, and how you can change them.

Published 2007 Revised 2009 Electronic version 2019

Stamp Out Stress

Living With Stress is a Choice, Not a Fact of Life

Description: By ending the war in your mind, you can manage the affairs of your life better. Practical tools for mind management

Published 2010 E-book 2019

Chakras Demystified

Our True Communication System Revealed!

Description: Practical information to understand how we communicate on each level of our being.

Electronically Published 2019

Healthy Children Only Need Three Things

Description: Practical insights and workable tools to enhance our skills in parenting.

Electronically Published 2019

Let's Get Hiking

A Guide For Serious Walkers and Hikers

Description: Practical information learned through experience

Published Electronically 2015 Revised 2019

The Ascenders Return To Grace Book 1

Magical Realism Fiction Published in e-book and paperback 2021

The Ascenders Return To Grace Book 2

Magical Realism Fiction Published E-book and paperback 2022

Mind Management Videos available on YouTube and www.montyritchings.com/videos

Conscious Mind Management

Living in Present Time

Quieting The Mind